As she entered the lodge, a man reluctantly cracked open his cell phone, touched a speed-dial number, and said, "The woman you asked me to watch? She's on her way into the lodge."

"For lunch?" snapped the voice of Tibor's shadowy partner.

The man sighed. "I think she's going to try for the upstairs rooms."

The cursing that came through the phone was so guttural that the man held the cell phone away from his ear. When it finished, he quickly held the phone close again and heard his boss say, "Follow her. If she tries to go upstairs, stop her."

"How do—"

"Whatever it takes. She's a small woman. Surely you can handle that much."

# ALSO BY TERRI DARLING

*Second Chances*

*What a Man Wants*

*Last One to Hide*

*Cinnamon Hearts*


COLLECTIONS

*Love Sneaks In*

*Love Sneaks In Again*

*Love Snuck*

*Love Steps Up*

*Love Steps Up Again*

*Love Steps Up Deluxe*

# TERRI DARLING

# Downhill Rush

*fiero*
PUBLISHING

Published in electronic form 2010 by Fiero Publishing
Published in trade paper 2014 by Fiero Publsihing
www.fieropublishing.com
Book and cover design copyright © 2014 by Fiero Publishing
Cover design by Terry Hayman/Fiero Publishing
Cover art copyright © 2010 mocker_bat/istock

ISBN-13: 978-1927920114

ISBN-10: 1927920116

First Print Edition: January 2014

For Melody, a better skier
than she believes she is.

# Downhill Rush

# 1

WHEN THE MAN KNOCKED ON THE DOOR of the downtown hotel room, his partner opened it. The man led in his latest conquest.

Without a word, the partner looked the dazed young woman over and grabbed her by the round chin to open her lips and check her teeth. The blond hair was next—it was tugged, the roots checked. Then the rear and breasts were squeezed to ensure they were natural.

"Okay," the partner said at last and stepped back. "She'll be the sixth."

The man who'd brought her in flipped back his own long hair and spoke with a Russian accent. "Good. Do you know how hard it is to find American girls who fit our requirements?"

The partner gave a crude laugh. "So taxing, I'm sure. You still don't think this is necessary, do you."

"If it works..." The Russian shrugged.

"It will. You watch. In three days we suddenly get the power you've been looking for. The girls are the key."

"We will see."

"And you?" the partner asked his blond captive, who had been blinking around with a dull expression since being led in. "Do you believe you will get everything you've ever wanted?"

The girl blinked hard, trying to focus on where the voice had come from. "Home?" she said wistfully.

Even the Russian laughed at that. "Not just yet, little *kroshka*," he said.

"Let's get her to the hills," said the partner.

The Russian nodded and took the girl's arm. But just before they left the room, the girl seemed to clear her head for a brief moment of lucid analysis. "Kylie?" she whimpered. "Kylie? Take me home."

# 2

THERE SHE WAS! The flash of dark blond hair. The small willowy body carving back and forth between the trees off the side of the ski hill beneath her. Samantha! It had to be. Maybe was?

Squinting down and backwards, Kylie Michaelson almost missed getting off the chairlift. Luckily one of the two snowboarders riding up with her elbowed her. She looked and jerked up her ski tips just in time. They hit the exit ramp and the boarders zipped down to the right to each strap in their free foot. Kylie slid, arms and ski poles waving madly, straight down the ramp and promptly fell over.

Blushing madly, she dragged herself quickly out of the exit path and managed to get to her feet. Okay, she thought, trying to steady her heart as she tugged up her gloves. Okay. Frosty morning air, overcast skies, crunchy snow. She remembered these from her childhood. She'd always hated them, but she remembered them. And skiing was like riding a bike. You never forgot.

Besides, she had no choice now. If that was truly Sam down there...

"Yo?" called one of the two snowboarders who'd come up the lift with her. He'd just finished strapping his free boot to his board and had rolled to his feet over to Kylie's right.

His companion answered with a whoop and they slid, faster and faster down the narrow trail that curved to the right.

Oh, jeez.

She brushed back her chestnut hair—it hadn't been cold enough to need a ski hat—and bent down to quickly double-check her bindings. Which is when one of skiers or snowboarders who'd come up the lift after her bumped her from behind and she started to slide forwards.

"Oh, no. No, no, no," she said as she waggled upright, her arms windmilling for balance.

*Just like riding a bike. Really.*

She was picking up speed, fighting to remember what she'd once known, when she noticed that as the lead-in trail approached the main slope, a small orange rope marked the out-of-bounds area along the left. Kylie was headed straight for it.

She was going to die.

Ensuring this, boarders and skiers who'd come up the lift behind her all seemed to be heading down at once, whooshing by her in sprays of powder. One clipped her on the left elbow and Kylie's left ski tip came up. Furiously she tried to compensate by pushing down with her right ski, but that just made the ski turn to the left underneath her. With a suppressed howl of frustration, she realized she was falling. Right into the path of a two more skiers.

Then suddenly she wasn't.

A hand had caught her by her right arm and swung it forward while an arm shot around her waist to bring her to an abrupt halt. She was panting, wild-eyed, in the intimate embrace of a tall drink of a man wearing a light, green-and-white ski jacket. He wore a Sherpa-style hat that wrapped around his face. All Kylie seemed to see was a chiseled, deep-tanned face that needed a shave, and eyes that were deep and hidden, but probing hers with an intensity that made her feel suddenly naked.

"Whoah," he said.

She wasn't sure whether her legs were holding her or only his hard body. And the air around them—it seemed to crackle and go very thin. Or was it just that she'd stopped breathing? It was hard to look at anything but the man's dark eyes.

Then he began to smile at her, a mocking smile, and she found her breath again. She pushed at him furiously. He kept his hands on her elbow but skidded just enough downslope from her so she could see he was on a snowboard.

A snowboard! Her parents had always told her that boards were for kids and snooty teens. They were totally uncontrollable, a hazard to the more responsible skiers, death to powder slopes, rebels and druggies all.

Of course, those were her parents' thoughts from the early days of snowboards at Telluride where Kylie's parents had taken Kylie and Sam learn to ski, but still.

She shook the elbow. "Let go of me!"

"You're sure?" He was definitely mocking her.

"Please." She made it colder than the mountain.

"All right."

He released his hold, and the sudden weightlessness she felt unbalanced her again so she began sliding forward to the lip of the narrow trail. Beyond its orange rope, she saw now, was a gully of tumbled, snow-covered boulders before the pine trees.

Her rescuer hopped like a spread-legged bunny up the hill to grab her a second time, but by this time some of her childhood ski legs had come back to her and she'd dug her downhill ski in hard, coming to an ungainly-but-effective halt.

"Good," said the man, his hand steady on her arm, tingling and annoying. "Now if you just bring the back of your left ski down a—"

"I've got it," Kylie said. Her face was red with humiliation.

Even worse, she suddenly realized, this man, this...overgrown rescue hero, had so distracted her from her missions that she'd completely lost her chance to catch Samantha on this run. Who knew where Sam would be by the time Kylie reached the bottom? Maybe this was just a quick morning ski for her, and now she'd be walking to some nearby hotel. Or driving out of this little ski development altogether; maybe driving back to Vancouver.

"I said I've got it," she said peevishly. "Thank you for your help. You can go."

"I can go?" he said. Laughing at her. But he released her arm and slid down a foot from her, not skiing away. Watching her.

"I mean it," she said, digging in her poles and pushing, sweating, back from the drop-off.

"Yes'm." Imitating something from *Gone with the Wind* now. He wasn't leaving.

Fine. Not only had he blown her chance to catch Samantha, now he needed proof that she could get down the hill without killing herself or taking out a dozen other people? With her teeth clenched and poles planted hard, Kylie, strained her way back to a downhill position. There she thrust her jaw forward, hunched her shoulders, and placed her skis into an ungainly-but- determined snowplow. Slowly, ever so slowly, she began a controlled descent around the curve of the trail.

Boarders and skiers, including two who looked to be about six years old, steered as far around her as they could, but she still felt a grim sense of pride. There was nothing, ever, that she hadn't been able to do when she set her mind to it.

"See?" she called back to her snowboarding rescue man.

With a swoosh, he was down beside her, sideslipping on his snowboard to exactly match her descent. His lips still had their mocking curve. His eyes watched her with fascination. But there were squint wrinkles around the eyes that put him at least into his thirties or even early forties. And snowboarding! A mid-life thing then. Probably married with kids. Seeking a little thrill in his life. Kylie had met enough of those in her job as a buyer down in Portland. Men eager for a quick fling to make them feel young and important. Kylie had actually fallen for one of them a few years ago. She'd let Richard string her along for almost three years, believed all his lies about getting a divorce, let him twist her heart into knots, before she'd finally found the internal resources to pull back.

Only to find that her baby sister had been getting into even worse trouble while Kylie had been messed up.

What was it about the Michaelson sisters that attracted such jerks? And why, so soon after she'd gained a more mature perspective on romance, was she once again feeling a tug of attraction here? Looks and snowboarding skill did not a good catch make. Especially when they distracted her from her mission.

She looked away from him, thrust out her jaw, and concentrated on getting down the hill.

"You're welcome," he said.

"What?" Kylie started at the nearness of his voice as he'd slid right up beside her, but kept her eyes determinedly ahead.

He laughed. "Macaulay Rush," he said and began sliding away from her.

"What?" she repeated, turning to watch, mortified by her sudden lack of verbal skills.

"My name!" he called back to her. "Take it slow and have a good time!"

Then he was onto the main slope and bulleting down the hill.

~~~~

Mac shook his head and wished he could smack it hard against something as he boarded away from Miss Fancy Pants. What in hell was he thinking? It was like his old rescue complex had jumped up from its grave the second he'd seen her struggling to get her rental skis on.

Something about the childlike jump of her nose married to a distinctly womanly body. Where had she gotten a ski suit these days that clung to her curves like that? Deep red, no less. And the determination in her eyes battling the fear... When he'd followed, then saved her from skiing into the gully, he'd been doubly hooked by the perfume she'd been wearing—light and breezy, expensive, as if she'd chosen it for the occasion. As if she'd carefully put together everything about herself.

She was trying so hard. For what? For whom? She looked like she'd been skiing alone, which was why he'd tried approaching her. But then she'd rebuffed him, something he wasn't used to.

Married, then? Attached? Lesbian? Work obsessed?

Mac shook his head hard a second time. Regardless, if there was one thing he was not going to do, it was get all wrapped up in a difficult woman. He'd been there, done that, had chosen a different course for his life that was working out just fine, thank you very much.

*Oh, yeah?* nagged a little voice inside him. *You're going to be blind to this too?* His head twitched backwards as he rode, pretending to follow the flight of the resort's sightseeing helicopter swooping back to its pad on the other mountain. Yes, Miss Fancy Pants was still there, stopped halfway up the hill from him.

*I'm surviving.*

Case closed. He had a snowboarding class to teach.

~~~~

Kylie saw her rescuer look back at her, then turn his lean body downhill and lean forward to pick up speed, jump moguls, and carve quickly around the trail's switchback down through the trees.

She chewed her upper lip and inwardly checked off all the errors she'd already made on this foray today. The most glaring one after overestimating her skiing ability was not asking her rescuer for information. He was obviously a regular at the hill, probably knew all the hills and maybe even a few of the people who came out here all the time. He should have been the first person she asked about Samantha.

But she'd been too proud and too wary of his interest in her. She'd behaved like a defensive schoolgirl or beauty queen. That might be acceptable behavior for a Nieman Marcus buyer, but it wasn't going to help her find her sister. She had to go back to the mode she'd been consciously developing since her search began. Think *open-minded, charming, questioning.*

Yet at the same time, *tough*. The man who her parents said had seduced Samantha away from university sounded dangerous. It had taken Kylie almost three days of asking around the University of Wisconsin where Sam had met the man to get his name, Mark Roskov. He apparently was sleek and gorgeous, with a hawk-like nose and jet black hair worn down to his shoulders.

Another day of asking turned up someone who thought Roskov had only been visiting Wisconsin; he'd originally come from BC, Canada. Kylie got on the internet to hire a private eye in Vancouver who discovered Mark Roskov did not exist. But someone matching his description had taken a business trip to Madison on the very days Roskov had been there. His name was Tibor Balakirev, the playboy scion of a wealthy Russian-Canadian family in the Vancouver Ports shipping industry.

"Traveling in secret?" Kylie had said. "Who does that sort of thing?"

She'd almost been able to hear the man's shrug over the phone line. "Russian mafia."

"Really," she'd insisted.

"Serious," he'd said. "So if you want me to probe any more, it's gonna cost."

Instead, over her parents' protests, Kylie had taken an indefinite sabbatical from work, bought a plane ticket, and flown to Vancouver in person. She'd gone to the elder Balakirev's offices to ask after the son but she'd gotten nowhere. A quick check through the white pages, though, had turned up Tibor's condo address. And though Tibor hadn't been there, one of his neighbors told her that through most of February Tibor could often be found at his "second home" in the mountains just north of Vancouver. It was an exclusive new ski village he was helping to develop, more extensive and self-contained than the local hills but closer than Whistler. Balakirev's consortium had named it Milaya Ridge.

Which was why Kylie was here now.

"Shit!" some kid yelled as he skidded a sharp turn on his snowboard just above her and missed her by inches.

Kylie took it as a cue to get moving.

She snowplowed carefully down this hill, designed to be the introductory run, and decided she had to relearn to ski before she went looking further for her sister. If the man she'd met near Tibor's Vancouver condo was right, Tibor came out here for days at a time. Loved to ski. All Kylie had to do was learn to maneuver these slopes, ask enough questions, and she'd at least find this possible mobster. Hopefully her sister would still be with him.

Kylie therefore headed for the same chairlift she'd first come up and flashed a dazzling smile at the young liftie who operated it. He was a few years older than the average liftie here, maybe all of twenty-two. Still too young for her, but hunky in a soap opera kind of way. Windswept blond hair he'd obviously spent some time on, but a refreshingly open country-boy manner, with the strong thighs of a regular skier or boarder.

"Made it down okay?" he asked as she slid into one of the four loading tracks, alone this time since the line had become less crowded.

She laughed and read his name tag. "Barely, Bo!"

"Well you keep right on trying," he said with what she guessed was meant to be his killer smile. His eyes ran obviously down and up her body.

Good. Kylie smiled to herself as the chair swung under her and she was away. She wasn't above flirting a bit to get an ally.

She'd ask him about Samantha soon. But first she had to relearn to ski!

And so she did.

For the next three hours she pushed herself relentlessly. She studied other skiers. She found ways to ride the chairlift up with the good ones and pumped them with questions on technique. She even accepted the offer of one older gentleman who skied down with her twice from the top and gave her pointers all the way.

Crouch, plant pole, spring up and swish around...

She passed Macaulay Rush a few times, surprised to see he was a snowboard instructor teaching a group of teens half his age, both boys and girls. Even from a distance, Kylie was struck again by the man's incredible sense of self-assurance, but even more by his apparent patience. When he came close to each kid to point out how they could improve, joking where needed, or serious and supporting, she saw no trace of mockery. Just caring.

Hm.

The third time, she caught his eye as she skied past to show him there were no hard feelings. He looked away like she didn't exist.

Of course. Of course. She deserved that. She'd been rude. Downright nasty. But *he* hadn't exactly been patient and caring with *her* now, had he?

Distracted by how mean he was being to her now, she missed a mogul, had it buck her suddenly, and went sprawling and spinning in a snowy mess down twenty feet of hill.

*Thank you, Mr. Rush*, she thought when she'd stopped. She wiped snow from her eyes and mouth. *Thank you very much.*

By noon, she'd progressed enough to try a few blue runs and came down them feeling pretty good. Yes, her thighs and bum ached from the unexpected demands and her feet were cramping from the ill-fitting rental boots, but the satisfaction of being able to actually look *good* from her imaginary bird's eye view, pushed all the aches away. She hoped Macaulay had noticed.

No. Wipe that thought.

How about—even her mother and father would be impressed? Sure. She decided against one more run up the beginner's chairlift and poled her way to the sprawling lodge for some lunch. Of course, if her parents had been impressed, it would have meant they'd seen her, which meant they'd have been up here looking for Samantha themselves. And that would have been too time consuming for them, wouldn't it. Too inconvenient.

The thought made her mood take a sudden dive and everything became harder. She reached the front of the lodge and skied awkwardly to the ski racks. A line of perspiration trickled down her temple as she looked down to stab her ski poles at her bindings to make them release.

Face it, she thought. So far all she'd really accomplished today was prove once again that she could do anything Samantha could by dint of sheer hard work. But she hadn't found Sam herself. There'd been no sign of her on the hills after all. The people on the chairlifts, mostly visitors, many German and Asian tourists, didn't recognize Samantha's picture. Bo-the-liftie swore he'd never seen Sam here but sure would have remembered if he had. "Almost as pretty as you," he'd gushed.

And now her bindings were not releasing.

"Argh!" she grunted and rammed her ski pole tips together into the snow. One stuck. The other fell over.

Forcing herself to ignore it, she bent over double to try releasing the right binding with her hands. It only unbalanced her so she began sliding. She hopped, skipped sideways, grabbed at the ski rack, missed...

Strong hands caught her under the arms from behind and pulled her upright. She didn't have to turn to know it was Macaulay's face she'd see smirking at her. It was like her whole body had somehow become sensitized to his touch and thrilled with eagerness to get more, even as her pride bristled. What? He only came to her when she was weak? She stared straight ahead, her face burning.

"Let me give you a hand," came his voice, warm and gravelly. His boot—he obviously had his snowboard off now—stomped down on the back of her right binding, springing her ski boot free. He still held her as he did the other one and she stepped completely free of the skis.

"You can let me go now," she said.

"You're sure?" With incredible audacity, he'd stepped closer to her and slid his hands forward under her arms so his own arms wrapped around her from behind. She didn't let men *do* that sort of thing. Other than her one mistake with Richard, it was always Kylie who was in control and calling the shots.

But through her jacket now Macaulay's arms pressed the undersides of her breasts and sent little shocks through her. Then his grizzled cheek trapped a wave of her hair against the left side of her face. She could feel his breath, hot and smelling like sweet coffee, and the rustle of his ski jacket, open and rubbing the sides of her own.

Kylie felt her knees shake and heart race so hard that her scalp tingled. She forced coolness into her voice. "I've been able to stand on my own two feet since I was a year old."

"I bet."

His hands suddenly released her and her body felt an urge to turn and grab them back again, an impulse that was so out of character it almost made her cry out.

He saved her by stepping fully away and to one side so she could see his face. That half smile, mocking her. It slapped Kylie's weakness away and she arched a brow at him.

"Are you trolling for business?" she asked.

"What?"

"You're a ski instructor, right? Or do you only do snowboarding? Do you get a commission if you bring a new student into the school for lessons?" She jabbed her ski pole toward the rental shop building just left of the lodge. A sign across the peak of it also announced it as the meeting place for ski or snowboarding lessons.

Macaulay's tan face flushed red. "This isn't my usual mountain. I'm only up here filling in as a favor to someone. So no, I don't get a 'commission' for bringing in new students."

Kylie was flustered by his anger but fought not to show it. "You're here as a favor? For whom? Tibor Balakirev?"

His face froze and his eyes tightened. "What do you know about Tibor?"

"Um...he's...a friend," she said.

"A friend."

"That's right." She licked her lips. Her mouth had gone very dry under his narrowed gaze. "Do you...uh...know where I can find him?"

A part of her hoped he'd burst out protectively that Tibor was a dangerous man and she had to stay away from him, but he didn't. Rush just stared at her a beat longer then tossed his head towards the second story of the ski lodge. The lodge looked like a high-end log cabin that had been stretched lengthwise double tiered at the northern end, far down from the main entrance where skiers and snowboarders stomped in and out. The steeply-sloped roofs were covered with snow that was melting back from the eves. Where Macaulay Rush was indicating was the second story at the northern end.

"I understand Tibor's got a private club up there," Rush said, "for all his girls."

The slight accent he put on the last word, the way his eyes flicked dismissively over Kylie's body as he said it, made Kylie blush. She recalled the descriptions of Tibor as a Russian lothario and her blush grew hot with indignation. She wanted to whip out her picture of her sister, show it to this man, and tell him *that* was who she was really looking for.

But two things suddenly struck her. First, this man obviously thought she'd be safe talking to Tibor so Tibor likely wasn't the Russian mobster her PI had believed. Second, if Rush thought, however rudely, that she was somehow the type who could be one of Tibor's "girls", then maybe others would too. It might ease her way to seeing Tibor himself. And that mission was more important than her pride right now.

So Kylie smiled tightly, nodded, and simply said, "Thank you."

Her answer made Rush's face go dark and he stepped definitively back from her.

He made no move to leave or walk with her into the lodge, so Kylie said, "What's good to eat in there?"

"Ask Tibor."

"Maybe I will," she snapped and clumped in that direction without looking back.

~~~~

As she entered the lodge, a man reluctantly cracked open his cell phone, touched a speed-dial number, and said, "The woman you asked me to watch? She's on her way into the lodge."

"For lunch?" snapped the voice of Tibor's shadowy partner.

The man sighed. "I think she's going to try for the upstairs rooms."

The cursing that came through the phone was so guttural that the man held the cell phone away from his ear. When it finished, he quickly held the phone close again and heard his boss say, "Follow her. If she tries to go upstairs, stop her."

"How do—"

"Whatever it takes. She's a small woman. Surely you can handle that much."

# 3

KYLIE PULLED OPEN one of the ski lodge's two front doors to a whoosh of hot air and noise from inside.

The dining area was ahead of her, a cavernous space milling with people chattering foot trays from the serving counter angled out through the middle of it, and shuffling and banging up and down from crowded, bench-seating tables. Lockers and washrooms were just to the right. An equipment boutique hummed with people up a few stairs past them, down a carpeted hallway that led to what looked like a theater or condominium sales office. (And some stairs to the second floor?) Everywhere looked jammed. Maybe it was the Russian influence, but the place seemed full of far more boisterous enjoyment than the ski lodges she remembered.

She snorted at herself. *The ski lodges she remembered.* Those were from almost twenty years ago. They were also the memories of a little girl who didn't want to be skiing at all, a girl already setting her mind and heart on a different path than the one her parents had laid out for her.

And now here she was, not only in a ski lodge, but planning

to invade its deep sexual secrets and find its sanctum sanctorum... in ski boots?

Kylie looked down, suddenly remembering the distress of her feet and clumped to over to a wall this time before bending down to unsnap her buckles and relieve the pressure. One advantage of snowboarding, she thought with a groan of pain as the boots loosened and she wiggled her toes inside them, was the boots looked a whole lot more comfortable.

A quick scan of the room showed a pretty even split between skiers and snowboarders, mostly identifiable by the boots they all still wore. Good. At least she wasn't out of place that way.

And she did need food, she realized suddenly. Her stomach was rumbling, her head felt faint. With a passion she normally reserved only for work (well, okay, for most things), she clumped to the serving counter, grabbed a tray, and joined the line of people ordering everything from chili dogs to grilled scallop and spinach fettuccini. Kylie grabbed a pre-made turkey sandwich and skim milk and skipped around most of them to pay at the register.

It was only when she'd found a table with space and was sitting beside down some teen boys scarfing down mixed green salads of all things, that the hair on her neck finally began to prickle.

She was being watched.

~~~~

The man who'd been given orders sat by the window two tables over. He watched his mark's head twitch up and look furtively around the room like she suspected something.

He knelt down to re-lace his boots.

19

When he straightened again, she'd given in to hunger and was devouring her sandwich. Also peppering her teenaged table companions with questions.

They pointed to the hallway by the door and made finger motions indicating the path to the stairs up, along with some kind of joke that got them both laughing so hard one of them knocked over his can of Coke.

Two minutes later Kylie Michaelson was done and standing. That was it? Her whole lunch break? What did this woman run on anyway? He'd watched her struggling from beginner to intermediate skier all morning, while she'd simultaneously pumped everyone she could for information about her sister and Tibor Balakirev. She was like the Energizer bunny. She just didn't stop.

Except that now, as she dumped the garbage from her tray in the trash and left the tray on top, as she turned towards the steps just inside the door with a determined set of her chin, she had to be stopped.

He rose from his chair.

~~~~

Kylie popped a breath mint and sucked it furiously as she clumped to the three stairs that led to the north wing of the lodge.

The tingling feeling of being watched hadn't vanished with her hunger. She felt like any second someone was going to grab her or shoot her or scream at her from across the room, pointing her out for everyone as a trespasser here. She wasn't one of them. She wasn't even a real skier. She was a fake! Stop her!

To her left, the clerks in the ski boutique looked up at her as she passed. Staring at her? Sneering at her?

She looked out the window to her right. Were the people out there stopping to watch as she walked towards the north end of the lodge?

Were there people following her?

Halfway down the hall, an alcove opened up to her left. In it sat, a highly coiffed woman in dark dress sat with a young couple and browsed through a portfolio of Milaya Ridge ski condos with them. Behind them a glass door led into what looked like more offices.

Just ahead to Kylie's right another door led outside where the sunlit snow shone almost painfully bright. She could take that door. She could retrieve her skis, do the easy blue runs, run into Samantha, discover that Sam was just vacationing here after all, that she'd just needed to get away from their mother and father like Kylie had. Tibor, Sam would say, was nothing. An excuse. And Kylie would say, I understand but *call* me next time so we don't worry, okay? Then they'd cry a little, laugh together like they had when they were kids and Kylie was virtually Sam's mother and father as well as sister. They'd ski the afternoon together then Kylie would drive back to Vancouver. She'd catch the next plane home.

It was possible.

Kylie reached the end of the hallway and stopped dead at the carved herringbone-oak door that took up most of the hall's width.

Reality check.

The door had no markings on it of any kind but screamed rich. It also screamed intimidation. A surveillance camera studied her from a bracket on the wall up to the side.

Kylie gulped but set her chin. Even if the door led to a den of Russian mobsters upstairs, what were they going to do to her? Nothing. They'd just brush her off like they had at the elder Balakirev's offices in downtown Vancouver.

And if they tried to drag her inside? She wished she'd bought a gun after she crossed the border, but this was Canada. It wasn't that easy. At least she had the personal defense course she'd taken at the gym. A woman who frequently traveled by herself had to be prepared.

She swallowed hard, stepped to the solid door, and reached for the door knob.

A hand grabbed her right arm.

With a shriek that jerked around the couple and saleslady in the condo alcove, Kylie spun at her attacker, stopping her left hand just short of gouging out his eyes.

It was Macaulay Rush!

He blinked at her, looked from her face to her clawed hand, then back to her face. "You want to see Tibor that badly?"

Her face flushed a deep crimson. Everyone in the hall was looking at her. "I'm...uh..." She stopped. "Why did you grab me? Are you following me?"

Rush let go of her arm and set his jaw. "I saw you going for the door. I just couldn't believe it. I couldn't let you do it."

"Do what?"

Rush looked around, rubbed his nose in embarrassment and leaned in close. "Prostitute yourself to Tibor," he said quietly. "I don't know what he told you or what you think he wants with you up there, but I've see other women give themselves to him. It never turns out well."

*It never turns out well?* She looked into Rush's eyes and saw how full of hurt they were. They'd seen too much, knew too much. A knot of sudden, deep fear for her sister plunged to the pit of her stomach. Samantha *was* caught, wasn't she. Or lost. Trapped.

And this man? Did he know where she was? Was that the real reason they'd been fated to meet?

"You don't even know my name," she said.

"Now there you've got me," he said. "You never introduced yourself."

"But you still followed me, rescued me. Three times now."

Again he looked embarrassed. But where the corporate types and salespeople she was used to dealing with would have either make a crude play or stammered and backed off, he just nodded and leaned closer. It was like he believed he could persuade her with just his energy field or sheer animal magnetism.

And maybe he could. Even as she was eager to find what he knew of Samantha, Kylie found herself staring at his lips, wondering what it would feel like to have the prickle around them rub her face as she kissed him. Wondering if his legs, hidden by baggy snowboard jacket and pants, were as thick and hard as she suspected.

"Look," he said quietly and moved her back towards the exit door, "I don't want you making a serious mistake. That's all. You look too smart, too...I don't know."

"Old?" She wasn't fishing for compliments. Samantha was almost six years younger and had always had rounder, doll-like features. Was that why Tibor had lured her off?

Rush seemed taken aback. "Hardly. As far as I can tell, Tibor's customers like them all ages and backgrounds. They just have to be pretty and willing."

"Wait. Hold it. What do you mean Tibor's 'customers?'"

He stared at her, hard. "You really don't know?"

"I really don't know."

"Then why did you want to see him?"

*Tell him!* her mind screamed. *He knows!* But some sixth sense made her hesitate. Even as her body was ready to push him back against the wall and rip off his jacket, explore what was underneath those baggy pants, the sixth sense observed that something about Macaulay Rush didn't gel. The troubled eyes. Speech and bearing far too confident for a snowboard instructor. He was hiding something.

"I'll make you a deal," she said. "Let's go somewhere we can talk. You tell me what you know about Tibor and his 'girls' and I'll tell you what I'm looking for."

There was a long pause as his gaze bored into her and Kylie felt suddenly naked. In a negotiation for a line of clothing, that would have been death. Here, it should have been worse. Kylie felt danger all around her. Russian mobsters, forced prostitution— that's what was being hinted at. Yet it didn't make her want to run. It made her nipples tighten and muscles quiver. . She remembered Rush's arms around her from behind when he'd caught her outside. Wanted to feel them there again.

"Okay," he said at last. "You drive up here? Parked in the lodge lot?"

She nodded.

"Go there. Change out of your ski boots. I'll meet you there in five minutes." He stepped to the door leading outside and swung it open for her.

She exited then turned. "Kylie Michaelson," she said.

"Hm?"

"My name."

"Right. Right. Five minutes." He let the door swing closed and watched until she walked away. When she looked back a second time, he was gone.

# 4

To Kylie's surprise, when Rush joined her out by her rented Grand Am, he didn't point up the street to the string of restaurants that served the little ski village. He told her to get in the car and head back out to the Sea to Sky Highway.

"Where are we going?" Kylie said.

"You want me to talk about Tibor, I'm not going to do it around here." He climbed in.

She hesitated, looking in the through the window at him. This man was dangerous, to her body or heart or both, but he was also her only lead. It was go with him or run back to the lodge and find a way to confront Tibor. But what if she just got stonewalled by Tibor's men, blocked out like she had been at the elder Balakirev's office?

No, the first thing she needed was information. She had to know what she was up against.

With a deep breath and her key ring clutched in her fist, keys poking out from between her fingers, she got into the car too.

Rush said nothing. When she started up the car, he directed her out to the Sea-to-Sky Highway and told her to head for

Vancouver, then selected a loud rock radio station. Her few attempts to draw him out—"Where's your snowboard?" "Left it. Have to come back tomorrow."—fell flat. So she just drove. She forcibly put all questions momentarily aside and absorbed the beauty of the shoreline they drove past. How had the 2010 Winter Olympic Committee ever considered not holding the Olympics up here because of this drive from Vancouver to Whistler? Even under overcast skies, the drive was a *selling* point. Kylie swore she saw two eagles and a hawk before they hit Horseshoe Bay and the busier traffic going along Vancouver's north shore.

When he directed her across the expansive Lion's Gate Bridge, then the smaller Burrard Bridge, winding through streets to where he said he had a waterfront house on what was called False Creek, questions ran riot in her mind again.

Foremost was: How does a snowboard instructor afford to own downtown waterfront in a west coast city whose real estate was even crazier than Seattle's?

There was also: Why had he been so uninterested in her name? Had he already known it? Had he been following her back at Milaya Ridge? And if so, why?

And last, most painful: Were her parents right that Kylie was plunging in over her head on this whole adventure? In fact, were their warnings the main reason she'd *had* to?

She forcibly pushed the last possibility out of her mind as Rush pointed her to a visitor's parking spot along what looked like a kitschy Fisherman's Wharf. The inlet here, False Creek, was like a great wide river that thrust into Vancouver, almost cutting off Stanley Park and its office building core from the rest of the commercial and residential districts. This wharf was on the south side of that inlet, looking across the water to the downtown high-rises, and beyond them the Burrard Inlet and north shore mountains where the sun was just breaking through the clouds and making the snow glitter. Stunning.

"Come on," Rush said.

He walked her along the elevated wharf's edge, then led her down a long ramp that descended to the water level. There, along the edge of the concrete walkway, was a community of maybe thirty tall, narrow, two-story houses, stretching two or three deep across the water. Floating, Kylie realized with a shock. They looked rock steady, all built of the usual west coast mix of concrete, wood, plaster, and glass, but they were floating. Narrow wooden sidewalks ran between them. Water lapped at their haunches.

Rush led her to the third sidewalk down and out along it to his house.

"It's like living on a boat," Kylie said in awe.

"Steadier," he said. He opened the door and waited. "Don't worry. It won't sink."

She nodded and walked in.

~~~~

Mac watched her walk past him, *felt* her go by, into his house, and his throat caught in a second of panic.

He'd had one or two women in here since Alyssa left him, but never anyone who'd affected him like this. She'd taken her ski pants off back at the resort to reveal form-fitting stretch pants on underneath. Between those and the tight, cream-colored turtleneck on top, Mac had no trouble understanding why Tabor might have plans for her. And did Mac really want to cross Tabor now? That could get him into a whole world of trouble, something he'd sworn his new life would have nothing of.

Yet here he was. And he definitely wasn't turning Kylie Michaelson away.

Feeling shaky, he followed her in, closed the door behind him, and studied her reaction to the place.

What he *had* forgotten was how playing with fire like this gave him a sense of exhilaration. The curves of Kylie's body and quickness of her face had him in thrall. They turned him back and forth to follow her like he was a puppet fixed by a wooden pin to the floor and she held the strings.

Not that she was Playboy-bunny outrageous or model thin like Alyssa had been, but there was a purpose to every movement and line of her. Ever step, every thrust of hip or elbow, every turn of her head. They seemed lit with an inner blaze, going precisely where she directed.

Except her dark hair, he thought, as she swept it back again from her face and tried to catch it behind her ear. He'd noticed that frequent motion even on the slopes and had longed to ask her why she didn't tie it back, wear a hat to hold it in place. Something. Except it seemed important to her. Maybe it represented her own little struggle between being wild or carefully controlled.

Part of her intrigue.

"Can I see the upstairs?" she asked and he snapped back on the defensive.

She was standing in the eating area that ran seamlessly off the living room on the north side of the house. Behind her was the floor-to-ceiling window that looked out over the water. It backlit her as she looked his way, making her glow but shadowing her face so he couldn't read her expression.

Did she like the place? Was she disgusted? Or a bit of both?

Alyssa, he remembered, had been enchanted when he'd first brought her here. But when she'd left, she'd screamed how this place was part and parcel of everything wrong about him.

"Sure," he said now. "Knock yourself out."

He thought he saw her give him an odd, startled look, then she was walking back through the living room to the narrow stairs and up.

Should he follow her? Should her try again what he'd almost been unable to stop himself doing out front of the Milaya Ridge lodge? He could put his arms around her. He knew she felt some of what he did. He'd felt her tremble. If he just went up now...

~~~~

As she stepped onto the second floor, Kylie felt the sudden need to tiptoe. It was as if the downstairs was Macaulay Rush's public persona—there seemed nothing there that spoke of *him*; everything was wood, rustic, tasteful but almost willfully bare; there were no photographs with people in them—while upstairs was his inner self. She'd felt it in his hesitation when she'd asked. And there'd been a strange catch in his voice when he'd said *Sure*.

The upstairs appeared to have three small bedrooms and a bathroom, with seemed a lot for a single man, living alone. As she peeked into what looked the master, Kylie saw why.

A opposite the queen-sized bed, on a light pine dresser, sat a framed picture in an ornate silver frame that seemed totally out of place with the rest of the furnishings. It showed Macaulay and a woman, shoulder to shoulder, head to head, smiling and flushed as they held up what looked like wine glasses. Macaulay looked younger in the photo, maybe in his twenties. The woman, black hair and dressed all in black, looked waifishly elegant. Her cheekbones were dramatic frames to a large mouth and flashing eyes. She was the sort of women, Kylie knew, whom men did double-takes to look at in a crowded room.

"My ex-wife," Macaulay said behind her, making her start.

She turned. The haunted look was back in his eyes as he looked at her even though he crackled with energy this close.

"She left you," Kylie said.

"In a manner of speaking."

"And you still haven't quite given her up."

One side of his mouth curved wryly up. "On the contrary, I keep the picture there to remind me every morning when I wake up all the things I'm fortunate enough to be free of."

There was bitterness behind the words, but not all directed at this woman. Kylie looked back at the picture. "What's her name?"

"It was Alyssa Rush. It still is Alyssa Rush. After dumping me, she married my younger brother."

Kylie shot him a quick look. "That must have hurt."

He held her gaze for a second, as if trying to decide something. Then he motioned for her to follow him. "Let me show you who I used to be."

He led her out of the master bedroom to the next door in the hall. He had to pull out his keychain to unlock it, and when he pushed it open, he had to shove back some document boxes stacked near the door before they could enter.

The room, obviously a home office, was jammed with these boxes. Two full-height cabinets also lined one wall. A third half-height one beside them held a laser printer that looked like it hadn't been used in a while. It, like the desk, the computer, the shelves of books along the opposite wall, and the stacks of files on the desk and floor, had a film of dust on them.

The little free wall space, on the wall to the right of the door, held a number of framed degrees, plaques, and photos. The largest degree was from the Law School of the University of British Columbia. The plaque beside it was an "Appreciation" for Macaulay's work done as President of the Trial Lawyers Association of BC.

"My brother, John, and I come from a long line of legal wonks," Macaulay said. "My dad was a Chief Justice. John does corporate. I, obviously, did litigation."

"Until...?"

"I got tired of it."

Kylie had stepped further into the cramped office to examine the rest of the picture wall. It was mostly photographs, many of smiling people in wheelchairs or disfigured in some way, many holding out their right arms, thumbs up. The cutest was the one down at the bottom on the left, almost as if Macaulay wanted it hard to see. It was of a young girl who reminded Kylie of Samantha, blond and happy. She was maybe thirteen years old, grinning ear to ear, and had obviously signed the picture herself. It said, "Thanks, Gunner." Signed: "Melanie."

"Gunner?"

He shrugged, still hovering by the door. "It was an aggressive line of work. That's part of what got to me. Only good thing it ever did was pay off this house and give me enough investments I can now afford to snowboard."

There was something very shaky under the words, worlds of things he wasn't saying. And now he was stepping out of the office and holding up his key. Like he wanted to lock it all away so it couldn't sneak out at night and bite him?

Despite her raging curiosity, Kylie nodded and moved to the door. But her ski pants caught for a second on a sharp corner of the office chair. She bent down to free it, and just as she was straightening to walk out, her eye caught one picture she'd missed.

Also low and semi-hidden on the wall, the picture was of a group of four men, young and old, arms around each other's shoulders. One of the two on the left was Macaulay. He had his right arm around a grinning man who could have been his younger twin. Obviously John.

Macaulay's other arm went around the beefy shoulders of a Eastern European-looking man in his sixties with a curving large nose and thin gray hair over a broad smile. That man's other arm went around a hawklike junior who looked too cool to smile and wore his jet-black hair down to his shoulders.

Kylie knew without asking that the two men standing with Macaulay and John were father and son. And she didn't think it was a stretch to give them a last name, either.

Balakirev.

# 5

TIBOR BALAKIREV HUNG UP THE PHONE from his silent partner in disgust. He tossed back his hair from his face, and turned to face the two men who stood like soldiers-in-waiting in front of his desk. They were brothers, Maksim and Slava. They made the custom-made Italian suits he ordered for them look like off-the-rack polyester, baggy and ill-fitting. But what could a person do? Some jobs required blunt men.

"The politician," he said. "This Jackson Pollard, and his aides—he has not given up. Now he is coming with his people to talk about the bear habitat on our second ridge. For the television. This afternoon." He waved a long hand in the air to regain his sense of control. and curled back his upper lip.

Maksim and Slava waited without interrupting. In this they showed the judgement and respect that Tibor valued.

"Someone must have told them this is when our delegation from Japan arrives. Someone is trying to sabotage this meeting."

Maksim and Slava still did not twitch, too stupid or loyal to feel the threat. Tibor nodded.

"Nothing must interfere with our meeting. Do you understand?"

Maksim, the older brother, cleared his throat. "You wish us to...stop Pollard?"

Tibor nodded. "Before he comes here. It must look like an accident."

Then he was standing up as if Maksim and Slava, bowing slightly and backing out, no longer existed. Tibor brushed down his suit and walked through the door to his right. The room on the other side was windowless, though the occasional whoop from the skiers and snowboarders outside would filter in.

The room's occupants were six young women, all between nineteen and twenty-six, all stunningly attractive and playing a game of poker on pillows on the floor in an almost frantic manner. "*See* your twenty and raise you ten," said the bobbed-cut redhead with enormous breasts.

"And I see you."

"Me too."

"Me too."

"See and raise thirty."

Raucous laughter. The addiction to methamphetamine did not make them intelligent players, but it did make them more sociable. And did away with any objections some of them had to remaining up here with him. The side effects—the leg jerks while sleeping, the compulsive house cleaning, the weight loss, openness to new sexual adventures—were all secondary to this unconscious devotion.

"Show! Show your cards!"

Yes, this afternoon he too would be showing his cards—his plans for a completed ski resort that would not only rival Whistler/ Blackcomb, but, almost a full hour closer to the Vancouver International Airport, become the power hub for the international jet set. The other players at the table, the six Japanese arriving this afternoon, they were the make-or-break bettors. They had been resistant so far, difficult to read, perhaps because Tibor wanted so much more than just money from them. *Which is why*, his partner had convinced him, *we must offer them more than money in return. You know how it's done.* And of course he did.

But these six had to be special, his partner said. Get rid of all the others. On all your business trips, be looking for these. Seek them out.

And Tibor had.

"Emma, you slut! You were bluffing!"

The girls he had finally settled on, seduced, and trapped here, could all ski, speak a number of languages (including Japanese), and had a natural ability to entertain men. *Geisha kroshkas*, Balakirev called them, crudely mixing Japanese and Russian. *Entertainer babies.*

Walking around the circle behind them, he ran a finger over the smooth jaw line of each, and each leaned into him like a cat as he did.

Candace, Emma, Neve, Toni, Galette, Samantha.

Tibor paused at Samantha. She was the only possible fly in the ointment. She'd changed her mind shortly after the plane had set down in Vancouver and Tibor had needed to give her a sedative to help her over that hump. And now her sister was looking for her. Whether Samantha herself had slipped out word, Tibor didn't know, but the sister had been asking questions. First at his father's offices, then at Tibor's downtown condominium, and finally here, at the resort itself.

Tibor's curled his fingers into Samantha's hair. If it weren't for the six Japanese arriving this afternoon, he would simply dispose of Samantha Michaelson now. Perhaps her sister along with her.

But the timing was too tight to change his plans. Besides, it was entirely possible the searching sister had left protections, alerted others. A sudden "accident" would look too suspicious.

No, he thought, easing his fingers out. The older sister was out of the way for now, and Samantha was as hooked as the others. Everything would go as planned.

If it didn't, well, there was always Maksim and Slava.

"Okay, girls," giggled Samantha. "Stakes are going up."

Yes, Balakirev thought. For everyone.

# 6

H E HAD HER BACK DOWNSTAIRS, thank God.

"You said you'd tell me everything you knew about Tibor Balakirev," she said. She sounded stiff and guarded.

"Hot cocoa?"

As Kylie hesitated, Mac began bustling around in the small kitchen, partially filling and plugging in the electric kettle, cleaning the dirty dishes he'd left in the sink. He had to occupy his hands, keep his thoughts steady. He'd invited her into his office. Why had he done that? To impress her? But she was as sharp as any female lawyer he'd been up against over the years. He'd known she'd picked up on the picture of him and John with the Balakirevs. Maybe he'd wanted her to. To force the issue of her own involvement with Tibor.

Why couldn't he just ask her?

"Tibor?" she prompted.

"You were going to tell me why you wanted to see him."

She looked at him sharply. "You first."

He considered trying to stare he down. He'd been good at that tactic once. Make the other side blink first. Until he'd seen how little that got him. Until he discovered the uselessness of it all. You just didn't have that much control over things. There was no point in fighting.

He sighed. "Yeah." The water was starting to boil.

He mixed the cocoa and walked out of the kitchen and handed her one of the mugs of steaming cocoa. She took it wordlessly and waited. He cradled his own mug in both his hands, stared out over the gray waters of False Creek and beyond. The clouds were lower over to the north shore. He guessed that the snow they'd been predicting in the mountains all week had finally hit.

"Tibor Balakirev," he said, "is a shrewd businessman masquerading as a playboy. He swoops around with his long hair, seducing women like other men hail taxis, but behind it all, he's put together a consortium of international investors to build Milaya Ridge in a mountain range that BC environmental groups thought would be untouchable for at least another century."

"So he's smart and good with women," Kylie said.

He looked back at her and saw she hadn't touched her cocoa. Mac sipped his own and nodded.

"Does that mean his 'women' are all with him voluntarily?"

"I think they start out that way."

"But you mentioned 'customers.' You implied he's some kind of pimp."

Mac tapped his mug with his forefinger, wanting so badly to ask her how *she* knew Tibor that he could barely contain himself. "I did imply that, didn't I."

"So?"

"Let's just say that Tibor has a reputation from other businesses he's run. And he wants Milaya Ridge to become a full service resort. So if he starts getting some high paying customers, particularly from out of the country, who are used to getting female entertainment, I have no doubt he'll provide it."

"Sex?"

Mac shrugged and frowned. She seemed pretty cool about that. His brother John seemed cool about that. How in hell had Mac himself gotten so out of step with the world?

Kylie stared at him for a moment then reached walked to the ski jacket she'd left by the door and reached into an inside pocket. She came out with a photograph and walked back to him with it. "My little sister. She's smart, speaks several languages, but not *life* smart. Rebel without a cause. You know?"

And the lights finally went on. It was her *sister* she wanted to see Tibor about.

Masking his sudden wash of relief, Mac took the photo and studied it. It showed a young woman, possibly still a teenager, with long, dirty blond hair, round cheeks, and a dimpled smile that made her look like she owned the world. The family resemblance to Kylie showed up mainly around the eyes and the strong chin.

"So?" Kylie pressed. "Do you recognize her?"

"Nope."

"You're sure."

"Kylie..." He understood her anger now. And even as he fought to hide the elation that Kylie hadn't been as foolish as he'd believed, he also saw the mingled fear and hope in her face. It clenched at his gut and dragged him back to earth. She was in serious need, real hurting, needing to know whether her sister was with Tibor or not. And twenty-two months ago Mac would have responded to that without thinking. He would have jumped on his white horse, sallied forth to fight for her.

Not now. He was done with rescuing.

"I pass dozens and dozens of girls on the slopes every week," he said and handed the picture back. "She could have been any one of them."

"Is she a Tibor girl?"

"I really can't say."

"Can't? Or won't?"

"What?"

Her eyes glittered. "Would you tell me if you knew?"

He snorted, sick about not helping but unwilling to admit it. "What? You think I'm in Tibor's inner circle? Maybe helping him run his little stable?"

"Are you?

Mac jerked back, self-disgust turning to anger. It was one thing to accuse him of fecklessness, but thinking he might actually be *helping* Tibor? How could consider that? After he'd brought her here? After he'd let her see the upstairs, tried to explain? "You think I'm a pimp."

Her face flushed but she chase him. "You work with the Balakirevs," she accused.

"I do."

"You work *for* them?"

He grimaced. "Yes."

"So?"

She was standing inches from him now, her face boring up at his, as tight with anger as his own. Without thinking, his arms snaked out around her and pulled her the last two inches while his lips dropped down hard on hers, finding them hot and dry, frozen in surprise.

Then, for just a second, she melted into his arms, her lips eagerly responding to his, her jaw opening, her tongue hot and urgent, darting into his mouth. It made his own head buzz, his heart pound.

There! Did she understand now? Did even he understand?

Suddenly she stiffened again and her arms struggled up between them, pushing him back. One of her knees came up, hitting hard into his thigh as he turned reflexively. He released her and she jumped back like a scalded cat. Her face blazed.

"You pig!" she said. "You're involved in kidnaping my sister and now you come on to me? And what was all this?" She waved her hands madly around to indicate his house, his stairs, maybe the hot cocoa. "Is this lessons from Tibor? Picking up women like other men pick up taxi cabs?"

Mac felt the ice shoot through him. The little hypocrite! The self-righteous little... He raised a hand. "Oh ta-a-a-xi."

Kylie stopped dead in the middle of his living room and glared at him. "You pig."

"You said that already."

Without another word, she spun and strode to the door. She grabbed the ski jacket and tugged it on, stuffing the photo of her sister back into its inner pocket. Then she opened his door and stomped out, slamming it behind her.

Mac let his control slip now and took deep, shuddering breaths, his anger shredding his gut. She was just like Alyssa, he thought. Just like every strong, self-centered, driven woman who would never stop until she...

He froze, not breathing.

Damn it.

Running to his door, he jerked it open just in time to hear her steps running along the wharf's edge higher up. "Kylie!" he shouted.

She didn't respond and he ran out after her.

He barely made the ramp leading up when he heard her car engine roar and tires screech away.

~~~~

In her car, Kylie fumed and banged her hand on the steering wheel as she drove. She turned into a dead end and saw she had to backtrack up the hill a few streets to get on the bridge.

She yelled with rage and pulled a U-turn, roaring out of the back street so fast she squealed as she turned the corner.

Why had she gone with that man? No, wrong question. Her motives had been good. Information. That was all.

Yeah? Then why had she let him kiss her? Because she had. She'd been begging for it. At least a part of her had. She knew herself well enough to see that. Recognized the pattern.

So she was attracted to another bad man. He might not be cheating on his wife this time, but he was clearly cheating on his life. Giving up law—what was that all about? And going to work for a couple of Russian mobsters? Pretending to be some kind of dropout hippy snowboard instructor?

Oh, Kylie. You sure do know how to pick them. So, do you attribute this to your lack of love growing up? You don't feel worthy so you have to hook up with lowlifes to punish yourself?

Those thoughts took her across the bridge and halfway into the Vancouver core. By the time she'd crossed over to the north shore and was heading back for Milaya Ridge, she'd finished beating herself up and had moved on.

That was how she'd risen to her position as one of the three top buyers with Nieman Marcus Seattle. She didn't let things keep her down. She put them behind her and charged ahead.

Which right now meant determining if Samantha truly was part of Tibor's "stable." She wouldn't have to confront Tibor about that. Someone at Milaya Ridge had to have seen Samantha if she was. Sam might even be out on the slopes. If Kylie could just confirm that, she could call in the police. She'd fabricate a call for help by Samantha if she had to. They could get a search warrant.

Up ahead the traffic was slowing. It could be the ferry line-up because she understood that half the ferries for Vancouver Island left just north of Vancouver off this same road. Or construction?

No. Up ahead she saw a rising cloud of black smoke, like something burning hot on the highway. A few minutes later a police officer in a bright orange vest waved her over behind a growing line of cars parked on the shoulder.

She rolled down her window and finally noticed it was snowing in wet, spitty clumps. "What's up?" she called to the cop.

"Three car pile-up, ma'am. A government mini-bus lost its breaks and flipped. Going to take awhile to clear it."

"Oh, my goodness. Any fatalities?"

The traffic cop looked back at her with sudden grief etched across his face. "Sorry. I can't say."

"Okay," Kylie said and pulled back inside her car. For some reason the awfulness of it felt like a personal warning. She rolled up the window again to block out the snow and smell of smoke.

~~~~

He drummed his fingers on his vehicle's steering wheel before pulling out his cell phone this time. He thought Kylie Michaelson had been taken care of. But here she was, heading back to Milaya

Ridge. He'd had to run a dozen red lights downtown to catch up to her.

And while the accident ahead had stopped her for now, she showed no signs of taking the turnaround that the police were offering. Therefore, he should call.

Or not.

If he called he'd just be told to stay with her, not move, like some trained little monkey. But it wasn't like she could slip away from him. He'd put a GPS bug into her car earlier. He'd know if she started to move. He could catch up to her easily on the Sea-to-Sky strip. Send any warnings if he needed to.

What a good boy he was.

He gnashed his teeth and slammed a fist on the steering wheel. Tibor, Tibor, Tibor. He was tired of everything Russian and wished he'd never gotten mixed up in this mess. Because since he'd met Kylie, he'd wanted to get close to her for her own sake. But this afternoon had made that difficult. He needed to take care of some things before he saw her again.

Waving to the police officer controlling the turnaround, he edge out of the side line-up, drove right past Kylie to join the cars cutting to other lane and back to Vancouver.

*Don't worry, lover*, he thought recklessly as he passed her. *I'll be back for you.*

~~~~

Sitting in her rented Grand Am, Kylie tried flipping through the radio stations but couldn't find anything she liked. When she gave up, she realized she had that tingle in the back of her neck again. Like she was being watched.

She whipped her head around to look at all the cars, SUVs, trucks, but then the feeling was gone.

Paranoia.

Or hope? Was she wishing that maybe Macaulay Rush had chased after her?

Except that if he had, he wasn't getting out his parked car to come up and talk with her, and that was too creepy to contemplate. The last thing she needed in her current situation was a stalker.

# 7

THE OFFICES OF RAPNEY, SMYTHE, WALKER, were in the prestigious ScotiaBank building at the corner of Seymour and Georgia. The law firm owned the top three floors and all the offices on the north and west sides had windows that looked out over Howe Sound, the north shore mountains, all the way to Vancouver Island on a clear day.

The south and east offices had the less spectacular views of the downtown core.

Mac knew this because his little brother, John, had an office on the south side but had big plans to move to an office on the north or west side. John always managed to tell Mac this within the first few sentences of any conversation.

Today, though, as Mac carefully checked his corduroy pants before sitting in one of John's brocaded client chairs, he saw John couldn't stop scowling. His younger brother's hand clenched a phone to his ear with white knuckles. His forehead beaded with sweat.

"I can't talk right now," he said curtly.

Mac half-rose from his chair. "Do you want me to—?"

John shook his head and waved him back down. "Well what do you expect me to do?" A pause. "No." Another pause. "Because?" John ground his teeth. "Goddamn it, Allie, he's going to owe me big time on this one."

He slammed the phone and swore again under his breath.

"That was Alyssa?" Mac said.

"Passing on a message from Tibor. He...and *she*...want me to basically drive up the highway to Milaya Ridge and subvert a bunch of police officers."

"For what purpose?"

John shook his head. "Some important investors. They're supposed to be meeting Tibor this afternoon, but some sort of accident on the Sea-to-Sky has them stuck in traffic. Stopped dead. I'm supposed to unstop them."

Mac grinned. "That would be interesting to watch."

John grimaced much as Mac would have done. "Meaning you'll come with me? Be my emotional backup?"

"Sure. What else are big brothers for?" And it let him kill two birds with one stone: have time for the talk with his brother, and get back to Milaya Ridge this afternoon.

"Okay." John let out a deep breath and Mac saw him look ruefully around his crowded office. John was in corporate law, so his files didn't pile up with the endless medical reports and overflowing employment records and witness statements Mac had been used to. But law was law. There was still a mountain of paper whether you were a courtroom fighter or backroom solicitor. It was only once you got partnership (and the coveted office on the north and west sides of the building) that you had enough space and secretarial help to keep your office looking like the ones people saw in movies and television.

"You know," John said as he grabbed his suit jacket and led Mac out through the warren of secretarial stations and cabinets, "when I bring home the completed deal at Milaya Ridge, I'm going to be sitting where Jerome is right now."

"North or west side?"

"The north." They were at the elevators and John hit the down button. "Then I can spend my days looking over the mountains towards the resort that made me a rich man."

Mac groaned inwardly. Even more when his brother added, "And I hate to do this, bro', but I promised to swing by Maxie's on Robson to pick up Alyssa on the way out."

~~~~

The greeting Alyssa gave him when Mac opened the door and climbed out on Robson, was cold. "Oh. Mac."

His response was colder. He motioned for her to put her shopping bags in the trunk, then pulled the front passenger seat forward so she could squeeze into the back. Mac averted his gaze as her skirt rode up her long, sheer legs climbing in. Then he climbed in and sat with his eyes staring rigidly forward.

John tapped his fingers on the steering wheel, looked from one to the other, then shook his head, punched on his sound system, and selected a CD to fill the silence.

"Onward," he said, and they drove.

~~~~

Kylie could not believe this. They'd obviously cleared enough of the crash to let one lane of traffic by, but with the long lines of cars that had become backed up in either direction, that meant dribbling through a few from one direction, then from the other. It was going to take her an hour to get by here. She wouldn't make it up to Milaya Ridge until almost dinnertime.

And now it was snowing steadily. Great.

A chorus of angry honking sounded behind her and she looked back to see a stretch limousine and BMW sports car roaring up the center line behind a police escort. The limo's rear windows were all blacked out, making it impossible to see who was getting the VIP treatment, but not so the BMW windows.

As the cars rushed past, Kylie gulped down a surge of cold anger. In the BMW's rear seat sat a vaguely familiar woman. Beautiful but angry. In the BMW's front passenger seat sat Macaulay Rush.

It took Kylie an hour and a half after that to get past the accident site—she didn't fault the cops for holding things up; the crashed bus was a smoldering heap of twisted scrap; nobody could have survived that—and get to Milaya Ridge. What little sunlight had come through the clouds earlier was vanished behind the snow though it was just past six and there was a good inch of new snow covering the winding climb to the resort. Slick roads. With her luck, Tibor and his cronies would all have left for the day. As would Samantha, if she'd ever been here at all.

But maybe that was for the best. There'd still be lots of people, many no doubt here for multi-day trips, staying in the resorts hotels or quickly-multiplying condo units. Maybe Kylie could just hang out around the tow lines and lodge and show Sam's picture around. Someone somewhere up here had to have seen her.

Again, if she'd ever truly been up here.

"Not like you've got a lot else to go on," she grumbled to

herself as she pulled slowly into the lodge parking lot. All she had for sure was that Tibor seemed to spend most of his time here, and Samantha was last seen leaving Madison on Tibor's arm. (Though, Kylie had been frustrated to discover, none of the airlines would confirm Samantha had actually boarded a plane with Tibor in the past month.)

It was always possible, as she'd daydreamed earlier, that Samantha *had* just used Tibor as an excuse to vanish. She'd always been flighty. On the surface she'd done everything her and Kylie's parents expected of her, but Samantha had confessed to Kylie that the parental control was driving her nuts. She'd dreamed of getting out like Kylie had done.

"Sam, Sam, Sam…" Kylie popped the trunk, climbed out, and began collecting her boots and ski gear from it. Even with the snow coming down, she wanted to option of trying the hills again. Her lift ticket was valid all day, including night skiing after all. And just maybe she'd bump into Macaulay up there somewhere. Up in the swirling snowflakes. Out of the glare of the floodlights where it was just the two of them…

"Forget it!" She slammed the trunk angrily.

"Okay!" said a voice behind her, shaken.

She spun around to find herself face-to-face with Bo, the lift attendant who'd encouraged her so much this morning. He still wore his sweatshirt and open ski jacket like it was forty degrees out, rather than below freezing. His blond hair looked freshly combed; his apologetic smile, like he'd just spilled his milk.

"Sorry," Kylie said. "Thinking about someone else."

"Oh."

"You going home for the day?"

"Actually, I'm done work, but Mondays I usually stick around here for dinner and then do some night skiing."

"Skiing?" said Kylie. "Not boarding?"

"You mean riding?" He gave her another aw-shucks smile at her confusion. "You call it 'riding' on a snowboard. Most of my friends got busted wrists and concussions from that. Besides, I'm training on that run, Back-Drop, off Schlatter most nights. Slalom course. Aiming for Worlds."

Kylie looked at him with new respect.

"Not tonight, though," He said quickly. "We don't train when the eyeline's sub-twenty."

"Of course," Kylie said gravely, as if she'd gotten that. They both laughed.

"So...um..." Bo ducked his head. "I was wondering if you wanted to join me for dinner, then skiing. I saw your car coming back and..." He let it trail off and looked at her hopefully.

Kylie cocked her head at him. He'd been interested enough in her to notice when she'd left and returned. Hm. Yes, he was young, but that also meant less complicated, right? No ex-wives and ex-lives skulking around in a sealed office upstairs. And all she really wanted right now was a friend who could help guide her around this ski resort, take her down some of the more difficult hills.

"Sure," she said.

"Great! Let me take your skis. We'll get you a locker up at the lodge." He looked over her equipment. "Have to buy you some goggles there too."

And it was done. So easy. Now that Bo had cleared this hurdle, his awkwardness tumbled away and he began chatting her up like a real pro. He got out of her where she'd learned to ski the first time, where she lived, how long she was visiting Vancouver for, *and* told his story and educational background—raised in the

Fraser Valley, pre-med at Simon Fraser University—before they'd even locked up her skis and boots and wandered down the street from the lodge for dinner.

All the lights in the village were on now. Floodlights made the hills look like blurry sheets shooting up into the sky. And the snow, while getting thicker, wasn't driving down. It was floating down in thick, romantic flakes. Similarly, the commercial strip they wandered down now was milling with happy people going out for dinner or drinks, window-shopping the closed-but-lit boutiques.

It all reminded Kylie of the only parts of her childhood ski trips she'd enjoyed. The magic of the night. Twinkling lights. Conversation. Laughter.

"Wait!" Kylie grabbed Bo's arm to make him stop. The restaurant they stood in front of was like something out of Charles Dickens. Unlike its sleeker neighbors, it squatted in heavy wood, small cross-hatched windows lined with snow, and flickering candles inside. Bo hesitated until she said she was buying. Then he sighed with relief and they went in together.

It was not cheap, but almost full. There had to be a reason, Kylie guessed. She was proved right when she decided to go fully with the flow and ordered herself a succulent plate of braised beef. It came with steamed green beans and new potatoes under a light dill cream sauce. She ate half of it and gave the rest to Bo, who'd already chomped through a half chicken breast and fries. They lingered over a half-liter of house red wine. A needed respite from the tension she'd been feeling ever since she'd come across the border looking for Samantha.

And if Bo wasn't a scintillating conversationalist, if he didn't make her tingle when he managed to touch her hand as they talked, at least he was pleasant to look at. She was sure he'd lied about the pre-med—the boy did not have the smarts—but his interest in her was clear and honest.

She ordered them a dish of orange sorbet and two spoons.

"This," Kylie said minutes later as they attacked it with long skinny spoons and let the tangy scoops melt on their tongues, "is how to show a girl a good time."

Bo looked over her left shoulder towards the door of the restaurant. "Uh-oh."

"What?"

"Jealous boyfriend at two o'clock."

Kylie spun in her chair to see Macaulay standing in the doorway, glowering at her. She pointedly looked away from him, angry at the rush of heat he made her feel. "He's not my boyfriend. I met him this morning. Around the same time I met you, in fact."

"Yeah?"

Bo's eyes had shifted and Kylie wasn't surprised when she looked again to find Macaulay standing at her left shoulder.

"Looking hard for your sister, I see," he said.

"Girl's gotta eat," she shot back.

"Hello, Bo," Macaulay said.

"Hey, Mac," said Bo.

Kylie scraped back her chair angrily. "Okay. Now that you two have that all sorted out, is there something I can do for you Mr. Rush, or did you just come by to check up on me?"

Macaulay looked down at her with his own eyes hard. "I found your car in the parking lot and came looking for you. You know who just showed up for one of Tibor's private parties?"

"Let me guess," Kylie shot back, "someone who came in a

stretch black limo?"

Macaulay looked taken aback, but then nodded. "Six Japanese men, definitely higher ups. They left Tibor's party about twenty minutes ago to go skiing. Each had a female companion with him."

A lance of ice cut down through Kylie's chest and she dropped all pretense of casualness. "And did you...? Were you with...? Was one of the females my sister?"

Macaulay shook his head, annoyed at her or himself she couldn't tell. "I wasn't at the party. I just saw them come out and take off. Possible one of them was your sister. Show me her picture again."

Kylie fumbled it out of her coat pocket and handed it over, her heart hammering. Macaulay studied it. So did Bo, leaning over the table to see.

Finally Macaulay shook his head. "I can't be sure. But I'm going to go riding up Schlatter and Blue Ribbon. I'll see if I can track them down. Can't be crowded up there. If we find her, maybe I can convince the person she's skiing with to give her up."

Kylie's heart leapt. Something in Macaulay's eyes made her believe it and she didn't want to even ask how, exactly, he'd do the convincing. "But...won't that get you into trouble?"

He shrugged, but his clenched jaw said that it would. So why was he doing it? He'd implied only this afternoon he had no interest in helping her.

Bo, still leaning over the table and examining the picture, suddenly spoke. "You really want to find your sister tonight, Kylie?"

"Yes," she said, almost choking as she turned to him.

"Then why don't I take you up the other two hills. We'll check those."

"In this weather?" Macaulay asked sharply.

"Not snowing that hard," said Bo.

"It's getting worse."

"I'll go," said Kylie, "but..." She looked back and forth between the two men. "How will we— If either of us sees her, how will we let the other know?"

Macaulay reached into his ski jacket and pulled out a cell phone. Bo reached into his jacket and pulled one out too. "You got a pen?" Macaulay asked him.

Bo blushed and shook his head.

"I do." Macaulay pulled one out of his jacket pocket and wrote his cell number on a matchbook he grabbed from the table, handed it to Bo. "Yours?" Bo gave it and Macaulay wrote it on a matchbook from the next table. He stuffed it into his same inner pocket where he kept his phone.

"So," Macaulay said, still pressed close enough to Kylie's left arm that she could feel his heat. Or was that her imagination, generated by the way he made her heart race? Damn him. "I guess maybe we'll cross paths at the lodge later."

Kylie nodded her head fervently. If tonight she could actually pry Samantha free of whatever stupidity she'd gotten herself into, Kylie could take her and run from this place before Macaulay laughed and told her it was all a trick and Kylie was now caught too.

Because Macaulay Rush worked for Tibor Balakirev. Kylie hadn't forgotten that.

"Okay, then," Bo said when Macaulay still didn't leave. "You get going. We'll see you around ten, or before if they close down the lifts early."

~~~~

"Uh-hunh," Mac heard himself grunt.

Then, because he couldn't do what he truly wanted to do, which was rip that little blond faker of a lift attendant out of his seat and goose-step him out the door, he nodded tightly to him and to Kylie, and walked out.

Damn, he thought as he stepped outside. He gasped a deep breath of the thin night air, let it out, and sucked in another. Damn it all.

As if having to sit through his brother's weasely talk at the Sea-to-Sky crash site hadn't been enough—*"Sergeant Entwright? John Rush. Yeah, yeah. We sat together at the ball last year. Right! Rapney, Smythe. Right. Always big supporters. But look, I need to ask you something..."* Or having Alyssa smile bitchily at him when he tried to follow her and John through the doors of Tibor's upper rooms.

No, what galled him was how he'd seen Kylie's car in the parking lot later and made himself put Tibor's upper room under surveillance for her. Just for a few minutes, he'd told himself. Because he really had to know for himself as well. And then he'd seen the girl who looked like Kylie's sister. And he couldn't just not find Kylie and tell her. But when he tracked Kylie down here like some dutiful puppy dog, what did he find?

Kylie playing footsie with Bo Rhinegold!

"Stupid!" He kicked the icy sidewalk.

It was just...Mac was worried about her. Bo Rhinegold had never seemed as safe as his farm boy act. Especially when the kid seemed to set his own work hours, have unlimited access at the Lodge, and spend more time skiing the slalom courses up on

Schlatter than doing anything else. He had something going on the side with Tibor, Mac was sure.

*Oh, cut the shit, Rush*, he snapped to himself. The truth was he just hated seeing Kylie Michaelson sitting with someone else. It drove him crazy. And it drove him crazy that it drove him crazy. He'd just come from seeing Alyssa again, after all. It was a reminder that Kylie had the same good looks, the same carefully-put-together appearance, the same sexy intensity when going after what she wanted. If Mac was smart, he'd drop the woman and run.

Only...Kylie *wasn't* Alyssa too. Kylie's sexual vibe seemed unplanned, almost unconscious. And the anger that snapped out of her wasn't for selfish reasons; it was because she was alone in a foreign country, fighting to find a kid sister who might not even want to be found.

Noble, in other words.

Damn it.

He shook his head, glanced back at the Boar Tusk where he could see Kylie paying for the meal inside, then up at the hills.

Would trying to find Kylie's sister get Mac into trouble with Tibor? Undoubtedly. But his arrangement with the Balakirevs had made that inevitable, hadn't it? When, not if.

Grimacing at how badly he was messing up his vow of a new, simpler life, he jogged back down Slalom Drive to the Lodge to get his board.

# 8

THE WIND WAS PICKING UP A BIT and hurling the snow at the hills by the tenth time Mac hit the bottom of Blue Ribbon crouched down sideways and going like a bullet.

The snow whistled past his goggles and snapped his clothes, but he didn't feel it. He was too upset. He was convinced now that it *had* been Kylie's sister he'd seen coming out of Tibor's loft. And he was beginning to believe both she and Kylie might be in some serious danger.

*Youch!* He ground his teeth and swerved onto the cut-off for Schlatter he'd almost missed with the poor visibility. The snow had gotten worse. He could see maybe thirty feet ahead, dropping to ten at times. Another source of danger to Sam and Kylie.

As he thumped over a rough spot, Mac tried to get his plan of action straight. The three Tibor girls he'd managed to pinpoint on Blue Ribbon, girls he was almost certain he'd seen come out at the same time as Samantha Michaelson, had each been closely following or leading a Japanese 'date.' The dates had all been twenty to thirty years older and flushed like they'd been pumped with Russian vodka before they'd been set loose. But the girls—the *women*, he corrected himself, since most looked at least twenty—had been positively wild-eyed. He'd seen the look in two or three of his old clients. The ones with drug problems or psychiatric breaks.

So if Kylie's sister was one of these, however voluntarily she'd joined Tibor to begin with, she might not be rational. The best Mac might get was a positive ID.

It could be enough.

He reached the quad chairlift at the bottom of Schlatter and slid into the singles line, quickly kicking his rear foot out of his snowboard binding. The runs at Milaya Ridge were divided between four main hills—Blue Ribbon, Schlatter, Presto, and Streak—which formed a box canyon horseshoe around the artificial village of Milaya Ridge itself. Mac had heard John mention that Tibor wanted to expand down the back side of Schaltter and take over that whole valley too. But in the meantime, the only ways to actually leave the canyon were via the winding road that led twenty miles out to Highway One, or by helicopter off the helipad on the east shoulder of Schlatter. So Kylie's sister had to still be here. He couldn't imagine one of the Japanese group would leave with the others still skiing.

Of course, they probably all had rooms in the Ridge Hotel. Damn.

Mac had reached the front of the singles line and ended up taking a quad by himself when the only other people in line waved him ahead.

As he swung gently up the mountain through the dark, he peered intently down at the only two lit runs on Schlatter. The one below and left of the tow was widest and easiest. Shadowy blurs of skiers and boarders were still zipping down it. The one off to the right, which was steeper, narrower, and tended to get scraped and icy, had only a single snowboarder picking his way down slowly.

Really, Mac considered, what were the chances that the Japanese guy who'd brought Kylie's sister out here to ski with him would still be up here? Even if he was drunk, this skiing couldn't have been fun. Maybe Mac should just go straight to the Ridge Hotel and ask there. Or maybe go straight to Tibor himself, demand to know just what the deal was with—

There!

Something about the distinctive pairing going by below—squat man, slender woman following close behind—and a flutter of hair from under a ski hat. It might be dirty blond.

Mac leaned forward and cupped his ski gloves around his mouth. "Sa-ma-a-a-an-tha!"

The words were whipped away by the wind, but he swore the woman heard him and turned her head. Then she and her lead were gone.

Mac looked around. He was a good thee minutes to the top of the lift, but there was a place just ahead where it came within fifteen feet of the ground up ahead, manageable if you knew what you were doing. And while jumping off a lift would normally get your resort privileges yanked, visibility was so bad that Mac doubted anyone would see him.

He quickly swung up the safety bar, then his dangling snowboard, and kicked in his free left foot.

~~~~

This was insane. Terrifying. Kylie could barely see the dips before she hit them or track where the edges of the ski run were. In self-defense, she switched to full-time snowplow and felt like a baby creeping down the hill. She lifted her goggles as she went and squinted through the driving snow.

Where was Bo?

He'd stuck by her for the first two runs, patient and gracious. Then he'd said he could quickly check out all the side runs double-time and rejoin her. She'd be okay, right? This was Presto, the beginner's hill. And the main point was to find her sister, right?

The crumb had taken off without even giving her the dignity of agreeing.

A tree loomed ahead of her and Kylie screamed. She dug in her right ski and turned left. That had to be the edge of the path! She'd almost skied right off the run!

Where was a good chauvinistic snowboard instructor to grab you when you needed him?

She slowed to a dead stop and pulled down her goggles again. No good. She lifted them and cupped her gloves around her eyes to see if that was any better. "Bo?!" she called down through the snowstorm. "*Bo!*"

~~~~

"You're doing what?" crackled the voice in the cell phone. Despite the transmitter on the top of Schlatter, the signal was so weak it threatened to vanish any second.

The man repeated his plan loudly into the phone, sure there was no one near him who could hear.

"Forget that!" crackled the voice. "Do you..." It broke up for a moment. "...her in. If she..." Another break. "...tragic accident...

her sister...now!"

Then it was gone. But he thought he'd caught the gist of it. The man frowned and snapped the cell phone shut, put it back into his jacket, and set off down the hill.

~~~~

Kylie had stood still too long. She'd lost track of which way the ski run went and now. The wind whipped snow from the hillside now as well as from the skies. Visibility was down to ten feet at best.

She swallowed. Which way to go? She'd heard a roaring snowmobile a while back. Maybe she should just stand here yell until someone came to pick her up.

She smacked her hands together to wake them up, wiped her dripping nose, then held her hands over her ears. Stupid not to have bought a hat along with the goggles. The wind had chilled things considerably, especially up on the hills, away from the vents of the shops and restaurants. And her Bolger ski suit, pretty as it was, had been bought with coastal skiing in mind; not overnight winter storming.

Waiting didn't seem like a good option.

Besides, she was *not* the sort who needed to be rescued, was she? She'd made it out of Madison, Wisconsin on her own. She could darn well get down a beginner ski run.

It was just...just... What if she skied the wrong way and ended up in the forest or going over some cliff? And the clock was ticking. If they shut down the lifts and turned out the floodlights before she found her way, she could stumble around here all—

The lights! Of course! She remembered the lights on Presto

came down in two strings, right and left sides of the run. If she could just navigate from light to light, she had to make it down.

Looking around, she could make out the glow of two spotlights, one that looked considerably lower than the other. She headed for that one.

~~~~

Mac was riding too fast for this weather but he didn't care. After a smooth drop from the chairlift, he'd bombed straight after where he thought he'd seen Kylie's sister going.

*Thwump! Thwump! Thwump!* He let his knees absorb the moguls that would have sent a less experienced boarder cartwheeling. Broken wrists. Spinal injuries.

Tree!

He leaned hard back towards the hill and whipped his heel down to carve right. Just missed it, popped up, and kept going.

Thirty seconds later he saw them, the shorter man and the woman he'd thought was Samantha. They were upslope to the right, back under the chairlift.

No one on the chairlift any more, Mac noted as he carved over to intercept them. They were shutting them down at last. About time.

Whipping to a stop in position, Mac watched the mismatched couple descend. The Japanese man came skiing down first, all red-faced swagger, his alcohol buzzing his brain too much to be sensibly scared. Mac slipped down right in front of him and yelled over the wind for him to stop.

He did, sloppily, and looked Mac over with an outthrust lower lip. His "date" picked her way down to stop more gracefully just upslope of him.

Mac's heart sank.

The date wasn't Kylie's sister. It was some big-chested woman with what looked like red hair tucked completely into her toque. She smiled widely at him and raised her voice over the wind to say, "You here to guide us down?"

The Japanese man, who was all of five foot six but squarely built and had a commanding presence, shook his head fiercely. "We find our own way!"

"You know the hill well?" Mac asked him, then repeated it because the wind had whipped the words away.

"We follow the lights," the man said and pointed a ski pole up at the chairlift lights above and below them.

"But the trail doesn't *follow* the chairlift ahead!" Mac said. "It curves around to the right, then back! You follow the lights much further you'll end up in a gully!"

The Japanese man looked frustrated, then leaned back to the redhead. She translated it into Japanese for him. He nodded curtly then glared at the tips of his skis, thinking hard. Finally, he looked up at Mac. "My name Sato Hachiuma. You guide us down." He gave a quick bow.

Mac looked from the man to the redhead, then quickly around at the white-out conditions. He'd lost Kylie's sister anyway.

"Let's go," he said.

~~~~

It felt like hours that Kylie had been snowplowing down, though it had probably been only thirty minutes or so since Bo had skied off and left her.

The light strategy seemed to be working in that Kylie hadn't steered off the trail into any potholes or cliffs, but her legs cramped with the strain of keeping her tips together in front, her edges digging in. Her ears, nose, chin, and lips were numb. Her ears ached from the constant howl of the wind. Her eyes felt like rings of pain from squinting through the snow.

If she didn't reach the bottom soon, she was going to just fall over and cry. And she'd *kill* Bo Rheingold if she ever saw him again. If she ever made it back to the lodge alive.

A little shriek to the left jolted her from her misery and she thought she saw another skier! A woman.

Then another. A man, no taller than the woman, laughing roughly.

"Hey!" Kylie called out, only to have it come out as a frozen squeak. She cleared her throat desperately and screamed as loud as she could, "*Hey!*"

The woman swished to a stop, as did the man, almost on top of her. The woman pointed in Kylie's direction. Together the two made their way over.

Kylie gasped when they arrived.

"Maruyama Jun," said the Japanese man after giving her an appreciative once-over. He bowed curtly from the waist, then indicated his female companion, a pretty Jewish looking woman who was chewing gum furiously as she grinned at Kylie. "This, Gah-lette."

~~~~

Ten minutes later, standing beside the lodge, the man watched Kylie take her skis off with her two escorts and he gnashed his teeth. The man was pointing to the second story of the lodge. Tibor's rooms. Kylie was nodding.

Damn.

There weren't supposed to have been any of Tibor's couples on Presto. That's why he'd let Kylie explore there. But leave it to Kylie to find the only couple that *had* gone. On a hill that was so whited-out they'd shut down the chairlift twenty minutes ago.

Double damn.

Not that he ever would have hurt Kylie, orders or no. He cared too much for her to do that. But he'd figured the storm would keep her tied up, break her spirit a little, make her more manageable.

Now here she was heading right into the dragon's lair.

Not good. Not good. Not good.

It was time for some very fast talking.

# 9

THE SEVEN OF THEM HAD ARRIVED at the north lodge door simultaneously.

Kylie, heart beating fast, had already been excited to not only meet, but be led down the hill by, one of Macaulay Rush's "Japanese higher-ups" and his date.

But as she fumbled off her skis with stiff fingers and shoved them into a snow-blown, almost-empty rack by the main door, Galette gave a little screech of delight. (Everything about her was screeches and giggles, all done with an almost-comical Bronx accent. It was made worse by dark hair that was too flippy, eyes too wide, devotion to Maruyama borderline psychotic.)

Over at the door were three other people—a stern-looking Japanese man, a chesty redhead, and a solid-looking Caucasian male with a snowboard. The sight of that last man made Kylie's numb-with-cold face flush involuntarily. She forced herself to clump over no faster than Maruyama, even though she wanted to run, throw herself into Macaulay's arms, and babble out to him the adventure she'd just endured.

Halfway there, a swish of snow that somehow managed to hit

her and not Maruyama, announced the arrival of Bo.

"There you are!" he said, jumping out of his skis without visibly releasing the binders.

Kylie stopped and gave him an icy smile. "Here I am."

He made to put his arms around her but thought twice when she held up her arms. "I was real worried," he gushed. "Soon as they said they were going to close the lift, I skied up and down Presto looking for you. Came back here to get the ski patrol. Thought you might have gone off the trail."

"I almost did."

"I know. I know. It was stupid, *stupid*, to leave you on your own like that. It was only for a run, I figured, but I must have missed you when I came down the next time. All that snow. Or you must have been really off to the side. Or..."

He was so obviously distraught, begging hard enough to have Maruyama frowning at him like he was a piece of frozen turd, that Kylie felt her anger melt. Besides, it had worked out, hadn't it? She'd not only met Galette and Maruyama, but had an invitation (on Galette's babbled insistence) to join them and the others up in Tibor's private rooms.

"It's...okay, Bo," she finally said, then repeated herself because of the wind. "I'm going upstairs with these two now."

She turned back to the door to find that Macaulay was right there now too and had overheard. She expected him to object, but instead he nodded, his mouth a thin line as he looked from her to Bo.

"That's great, Kylie. Sato-san,"—Macaulay indicated the stern-faced Japanese man whom she now saw was older than most of the others, in his fifties at least—"has just invited me up too."

Mac's eyes didn't leave Bo as he said it. For just a second, Kylie thought he saw the younger man's eyes flash with something that might have been jealously, then Bo nodded.

"Sure, I guess. Can I...?" He looked at Maruyama, but the Japanese's frown grew even deeper on his face, like a dark woodcutting.

"It's *private!*" Galette sang out at Kylie's shoulder. "'P'—double 'r'—'i'. Sorry, toots!"

Bo nodded, faded back into the blowing snow, and Kylie was heading for the herringbone door with the rest.

~~~~

"Why isn't she dead?" hissed the partner.

Tibor shrugged and shook back his hair. He too was angry, but his pride did not let him show this. His personally picked man had failed him, gone his own way, and even been foolish enough to call and report this rather than running for his life.

He would be dealt with. But first, the woman. This entire operation was threatened by one foolish, brown-haired woman looking for her sister.

"We cannot kill her now," he said.

"Of course not," the partner snapped. "She's Maruyama's 'guest.' Insult her and we insult his honor. But she can't come up here either."

"I will deal with it."

"How?"

His broad lips stretched back and he looked at the monitor showing the couples who stood outside the herringbone door, requesting admission. The signs were all there. "You may listen. And learn."

~~~~

To Kylie's surprise, the herringbone door clicked open readily when Galette knocked a little "shave-and-a-haircut" rhythm on it.

Kylie glance up at the surveillance camera. Hadn't Tibor seen her? Didn't he know?

But then, why would he? Maybe all her tingles about being followed were so much paranoia. Nobody knew her here. She was just a resort patron, another pretty "girl" Tibor might use. Wasn't that what Macaulay had originally thought she was?

Macaulay.

He was pressed up behind her now, his hands protectively on her hips. It felt good. She'd have to scold him about it later perhaps, remind him she'd gotten her invite to Tibor's room all by herself. But knowing he was keeping track of her location this way through this steady touch, felt...good.

The stairs inside were just wide enough for two people to climb abreast. Not surprisingly, they ascended as couples, putting Macaulay beside her as the middle couple, his arm still around her waist. Her shoulder, she noted, fit neatly into the snug of his shoulder. And whether by unconscious attempt or divine design, they seemed to climb the stairs almost as one. Smells of cooked meat and a muted tambourine beat tumbled down from above, and Kylie found herself and Macaulay climbing in rhythm to it.

She became so mesmerized by the wonder of that, the movement of Macaulay's strong thigh beside her own, that she reached the top with a little "Oh!" of surprise.

There was a second thick door. Macaulay's Japanese host, something-or-other Sato, had led the way and now pulled open the door with an imperious flourish to fill the stairwell with dancing light, smells of sizzling pork and potatoes, and the driving beat of balalaikas.

It was like a sixteenth century Russian *dacha*. A huge wooden fireplace blazed in the northwest corner of an enormous room. A table heaped high with roasted meats, vegetables, fruits, and pastries of every description ran along the wall near the door. Kylie saw no live band, but the heavy wooden furniture, as deeply colored as the wall tapestries, shook and throbbed to the music and the dancing of the revelers. Japanese—Kylie counted five. Each had a young woman with him. There were also a Caucasian man and woman in one corner. The man was dressed in Ralph Lauren and looked vaguely familiar. The woman too, in what looked like a Dolce & Gabbana chiffon spaghetti strap that—

"Welcome!" said a tall, thin man, stepping in front of her. He shook back long black hair from his face and spread his arms wide with a smile. "*Kak-vehza-vice!*"

Kylie took a step back. The man's eyes were drinking her in, studying her like a predator so that Kylie felt suddenly naked, frightened and excited all at once. She felt her skin tingle as she understood. This was the man who'd seduced her sister, who'd probably seduced all the young women in this room so thoroughly they now worked for him. The man's hawk-like nose, the thin, mobile lips—this was Tibor Balakirev.

He confirmed it as he gave both of his returning Japanese guests formal bows and made a clipped speech about hoping they'd managed well on the slopes despite the weather. Galette translated quickly, the flawless-sounding Japanese spilling out of her mouth so naturally that Kylie wondered if it was the Bronx-ese that was the foreign language.

Tibor waved his returning guests to the spread of food and invited them to take off their ski boots, lay down their coats. As he did, Kylie saw the Caucasian couple watching her closely and that part of the situation finally twigged. The woman was Macaulay's ex-wife! Which meant the younger man with her had to be Macaulay's brother. And their relationship to Tibor?

Before Kylie could even guess, Tibor had turned back to her so forcefully she had to respond. He reached for her hand and she found it rising to meet his.

"Beautiful lady," Tibor said, "will you tell me your name?"

Kylie felt the man's power. It wasn't a good power, not the rush of filled senses that Macaulay gave her, but more the focused threat of a snake. Her whole being danced with adrenaline. She felt like she was leaning forward on her toes and worried that any second her trained defense mechanism might make her strike out and kick this man. "I'm...um..."

Macaulay's hand was suddenly around her waist again, breaking Tibor's hold on her. "This is Kylie Andrews," he lied breezily. "Kylie? Tibor Balakirev, owner of Milaya Ridge."

Kylie saw the Russian covered his flicker of annoyance with a smile. "Myself and the dozen other investors, yes?"

He released her hand and Kylie felt a cold rush of release that came out as a laugh. Yet her body still thrummed, every sense geared to surveying the room itself now from the corners of her eyes. Besides the entrance, there were six doors. Two doors were on the wall to the left, two on the far wall, two more on the right-hand wall. Samantha had to be through one of those doors or down the hall. She certainly wasn't in here. How big was the rest of this level? She tried matching this interior space against her image of the lodge's second story. She had to have seen it forty times today as she'd gone up and down the hills, but she couldn't do it. *Come on, Kylie.*

"It's an amazing resort," she said. "Among the best I've seen."

"You've been to many?" said Tibor.

"Telluride, Aspen mainly," Kylie admitted. "As a child. Many others through catalogue shoots."

"Yet you came here."

"Ouch!" Kylie looked down quickly at her ski boots. "You'll have to forgive me. My feet are killing me, but I left my comfortable boots in a locker down at the main lodge."

"What am I thinking?" Tibor said. He clapped his hands over his head and a large man in an ill-fitting suit appeared at his side. "Maksim, this woman needs a pair of aprés ski slippers. And help her with her boots."

The thick-necked man nodded and promptly fell to his knees in front of Kylie, unsnapping the stiff buckles of her right ski boot like they were licorice strands. He grunted for her to lift her foot, and when she did, he cracked open the front tongue of the boot and slid it off with barely a tug. Before Kylie could express her surprise, he'd slipped on a rubber-soled felt slipper he'd pulled out of somewhere, put her foot down on the ground, and went for the other boot.

Kylie almost giggled over the relief it gave her and she leaned foolishly into Macaulay. "Ohh," she groaned. "That is so much better."

"And now," Tibor said smoothly, "Maksim will accompany you both downstairs to get your own 'comfortable' boots. Unfortunately this is a private party. We have business to discuss."

"But..." Kylie looked around quickly. "Can I just use your facilities before I go?"

"Pardon?"

"She needs to use the washroom," Macaulay said.

"Of course."

Before he could point to a door, Kylie set off quickly for the right hand door on the wall behind where Macaulay's ex-wife sat. A drunk Japanese had banged on it a moment ago and been turned curtly away by Maksim's twin, Slava. Maybe that meant Samantha was—

A hand gripped her shoulder firmly. "The washroom is that one," said Balakirev and pointed to the door on the other wall.

"Oh. Oh, of course," Kylie said. She knew somehow that when she emerged, Slava would be standing in front of the forbidden door and Macaulay's wife would be laughing at her.

# 10

YOU PRESUME MUCH," Tibor grated when Kylie had disappeared.

Macaulay shrugged it off. He'd dealt with bullies and bluster his entire legal career. True, most of them didn't have a six foot, three hundred pound bodyguard standing behind them with an obvious bulge under their jackets for their shoulder holsters. But the technique for dealing with them was the same.

Stick to the strong facts. Bluff the rest.

"She was invited up by that guy, not me. Sato-san demanded I come up."

He caught Alyssa's gaze as he said it and gave her a little nod. She looked away, furious. John, beside her gave him the trademark Rush grimace and shrugged.

"I will talk with Maruyama and Sato," Tibor said, annoyed that Mac's focus had wandered. "You will take her and leave."

"To where exactly?" said Mac. "You've been watching the snowfall. No way anyone's getting out of here tonight."

Tibor's face was growing red. "Get her a room."

"Hey, you know, I checked that out earlier. But since you scheduled the redesign on the Ridge Hotel, its rooms are all gone.

I could get her into one of those hillside condos maybe. Of course that would put her right beside where your Japanese guests are staying."

Tibor raised a hand and Maksim, was there again. "You will accompany Mr. Rush and his woman down to the lodge for their things," he snapped. "Then take them to the Creekside Retreat. Put them in a studio suite with our compliments."

He looked coldly at Mac. "Will that do?"

"Sure!" Mac said. "I should be able to keep her out of your hair quite nicely there."

"See that you do."

Over the next five minutes Tibor circulated among his guests; Alyssa, whom Mac had to admit still looked icily stunning, studiously looked everywhere but at Mac. While Kylie, Mac assumed, was going through every possible way she might get into the forbidden room, short of kicking her way through the side walls of the bathroom.

Then Kylie emerged. She looked radiant.

Here was a woman who'd just been abandoned in a blizzard, rescued by what looked like a Japanese mobster who spoke no English, dragged up before the one man she wanted to find (but really should be hiding from), then had the one opened door she'd found slammed in her face.

And she looked...yummy.

Her luxurious chestnut hair, that had become flattened in the blizzard and drenched as the snow melted, had been dried and fluffed so it floated around her head, screaming *Touch me*. Her eyes, so often snapping mad at him, were sparkling with a mix of nervous hope and fear. And the combination of felt slippers and form-fitting ski suit made her look strangely helpless.

Mac wanted to run over, smooth down that glorious hair and sweep her into his arms.

She caught his eyes, her own lit up, and she tried to subtly indicate the door just to her right, the one Slava was now standing outside. Mac nodded. The fact the thug had been posted for their benefit did seem to confirm Kylie's sister was here. But this moment wasn't the time to go after her.

Mac crooked a finger at her to come to him. She looked puzzled, but did. When he told her where they were going, she frowned even harder. "But..." she said. "But...if Samantha's here now, maybe your ex-wife, or your brother..."

He raised a hand to make a shushing sound. Tibor was sending Maksim over to them. "Not going to happen right now. But no one's leaving the resort tonight. And we need a plan."

Her eyes sparked again and he felt like a fraud. The only plan he truly cared about this moment was getting Kylie to safety. And alone with him.

"We will leave now," said Maskim, and pointed them to the door.

~~~~

Kylie was giddy with excitement, so much she found herself speaking faster and faster as they came down the stairs and out along the passageway to the still noisy main lodge. "I rented the boots, skis, and poles in town you know. For the week. In Vancouver. A place close to my hotel on Robson? You never know what a ski hills selection will be like. That's what they told me. And it's more flexible? You can come and go. Well," she laughed and waved her hand at the swirling blizzard outside the window, "normally you can come and go!"

She barely noted Macaulay's nods or Maksim's lack of them. It was just a screen to cover her whirring brain.

A plan! Macaulay was going to make a plan with her! Which meant he was going to help her. Which meant that, a) he was neither a heartless bad guy nor a lazy schmuck; and b) she had at least doubled her chances of actually getting Samantha out of here.

And Samantha *was* here. She *was* in danger. Otherwise why would Tibor Balakirev be pulling all these strong-arm tactics to keep Kylie away from his back room?

*Lots of reasons—drugs, legitimate business. You didn't even tell him your proper name.*

The doubts made her stutter, but Macaulay caught her arm.

They were at the lockers. She fumbled out her key, retrieved her boots, and put them on. Macaulay got her skis and poles from where she'd left them outside. Maksim carried her ski boots. Together they plunged out into the snow to this place Macaulay had said he'd arranged for her.

Normally, she guessed, it would have been a scenic walk. Every part of Milaya Ridge boasted beauty of one sort or the other. But the snow was still whipping down off the mountains so fiercely that it was all Kylie could do to keep the pull-out hood wrapped around her head and keep up with Maksim's hulking figure in front.

At one point she wondered if she and Macaulay should just lope sideways away from Maksim. In this snow it might take the big Russian a few minutes before he even noticed they were gone.

Then Macaulay, who seemed to be getting increasingly psychic, shook his head at her and motioned for her to keep walking.

Yes. Because how exactly would she rescue Sam on a night like this anyway? Even if she could somehow sneak her out of Tibor's place, where could they hide? How could Kylie smuggle her past Tibor's people once the snow let up? There was just the one road in.

She sure hoped Macaulay had some better ideas.

Her ears, face, and fingers were going numb by the time Maksim opened the door on the brightly-lit lobby of a low-rise building whose edges were obscured in the storm.

The three of them tromped in, Macaulay set Kylie's skis against the wall, and he and Kylie spent a good ten seconds chuffing and shaking all the accumulated snow off themselves.

"Ms. Andrews? Mr. Rush? Your suite is waiting."

Kylie looked up, confused, at the diminutive male concierge who'd come out from behind his small desk. Andrews? Then she recalled Macaulay had introduced her to Tibor as Kylie Andrews.

But...*their* suite?

Macaulay nodded and held out his hand for the key card, took it, and turned to Maksim. "You can put down the boots now, big guy. And thank you. You can go."

The Russian narrowed his eyes at him and drew down the corners of his mouth, but he finally did as Macaulay directed. Just before he plunged out the door, Kylie ran to him and caught him by the sleeve. "Really," she said, embarrassed. "Thank you for carrying my things."

Maksim frowned again but gave her a curt nod and stomped out into the storm.

The concierge, in the meantime, had gathered up Kylie's boots and took them into a back room. Then her skis and poles. He returned from the second trip with a little claim tag. "You can pick these up whenever you need them," he said primly and smiled.

"Thank you, too," said Kylie and fumbled into her ski jacket for a tip.

The concierge smiled and snapped up a hand. "Please. Mr. Balakirev simply asks that you enjoy your stay with us. There's complimentary chocolate, champagne, and strawberries in your suite. Room service should you desire. Each suite has a gas fireplace. Our internet connections are unfortunately not hooked up as yet, but we do have full satellite television and movie programming. Perhaps this will replace the lack of moonlit views from the veranda."

"Oh my gosh," breathed Kylie.

Macaulay looked at her. "Did you just say, 'Oh my gosh'?"

The concierge beamed. "The suite is through that door, up the stairs, and down the hall to the left."

"To the left," said Kylie.

Macaulay rolled his eyes. "Come on."

Two minutes later, they both had their boots and ski jackets off, his and hers, in the little closet alcove just inside the door of the suite. The main switch turned on some pot-lights and they saw the suite was a studio affair, everything in one room, but the ceiling was double-height with one entire wall a high sloped window like a gilded frame to the silent blizzard outside. Kylie craned her head around, wide-eyed.

The wall to the right had a fireplace and television unit, fresh plants in wall hangers, a door to the bathroom. The central space had a small oak table and chairs near the window, a set of overstuffed velour love seats with a coffee table nearer the door.

The left wall had a kitchenette in brushed metal and a steep flight of oak stairs on the far side that led up over it. At the top of the stairs was a half-height wall, a loft looking down onto the main area. That had to be the bedroom.

"Right," said Kylie as she forced herself to walk further in on the broadloom. "The question is how we're going to get Samantha away from the others. And whether Tibor would actually try to"—she ran her fingers over the velour of the love seats, had a sudden image of her and Macaulay on them, jerked her hand back—"stop us with force. We could try calling in the police, of course."

She stopped at the bottom of the stairs. Licking her dry lips, she gripped the railing, and climbed the stairs quickly. Yup. There it was. One queen-sized bed. Only the indirect light from the pot-lights downstairs. She turned and hurried back down the stairs to where Macaulay stood in the center of the room, his eyes following her.

"Of course the police wouldn't be able to make it out here until tomorrow afternoon," Kylie said quickly. She turned from his gaze to look hard out the window at the snow. "But if we called them, they could follow the snowplows up."

There was a slight scuffing sound and Macaulay was suddenly behind her. His body burned like a furnace. The heat of it enveloped her back, licked its way somehow around her thighs and spread upward.

She broke forwards and walked over to the little eating table and chairs. It was blond wood, the corners rounded. In the middle of it reclined a basket of individually wrapped chocolates, a silver ice bucket with the sweating bottle of champagne, and a crystal bowl holding a small ring of oversized, perfect strawberries. Ripe. Red.

"I wonder if the fireplace works when the electricity fails?" she said.

"Probably." He had walked up beside her, put his fingertips on the table beside hers.

She turned to go to the fireplace, but his fingers caught her hand, forcing a little breath out of her. Then he pulled and it was like he was reaching inside her, pulling her from somewhere under just under her navel. Her feet turned of their own accord. Her legs moved in towards his. Her hands came up feebly beside her breasts.

"You...don't have your own place here," she said.

He shook her head. "I'm stranded. Like you."

She swallowed.

He was just that much taller than her, and stronger, that when his arms went around her back, slid down and pressed her closer, she seemed to sink onto his chest. Her breasts pressed into him like a sigh. Her fingers spread against the rough cotton of his sweatshirt, felt the hardness of the muscle there. The hardness all up and down his body.

"I can't," she whispered.

"Really?"

One of his strong hands suddenly had her by the back of her head, supporting it as she tilted it back, and his lips came down to her like an irresistible cosmic force.

There was no stiffness when they met this time. His lips brushed hers once, twice. Then hers and his slid together, opening eagerly, tongues meeting and tasting, slipping against each other hot and soft. He tasted like fire and smoked meat, as if he'd sampled some of Tibor's buffet spread earlier. Or perhaps it was just him, burning up inside like Kylie felt herself burning.

She could feel her heart pounding against him as if it wanted to join him, suck his heat into her, give him all of her own.

Unconsciously Kylie slid her hands up from his chest and around his neck.

# 11

As Kylie's fingers wrapped into the hair at the nape of his neck, Mac groaned. His whole body shook, trembled with something so far beyond his experience that it scared him.

He'd known this was coming when he'd led Kylie in here. Hell, he'd planned it from the moment she'd slipped into the washroom in Tibor's upper rooms and he'd been alone with the Russian.

What he hadn't planned was how the fact of it so overwhelmed him. It worried him. He should stop and draw back.

But when they separated their lips for a second, Kylie breathed, "Macaulay," and that was it for him. In a move he would have reviled as crass macho posturing even a day earlier, he pulled her fingers from around his neck and reached down to physically sweep her up in his arms, like a groom about to carry his bride over the threshold.

He expected laughter, but saw only flared nostrils and burning eyes when he looked at her face. A definite green light.

Careful not to bang her head, he swung her around and walked with the strength of ten men to the bottom of the stairs leading to the loft. There he stopped. It was too narrow to carry her up as they were. He began to swing her sideways.

"Set me down," she said thickly.

Heart banging on the verge of shouting *NO*, he let her slip to the floor, her ski pants swishing down against his own. Then she grabbed one of his hot hands and started up the stairs, pulling him up behind her.

*Complicated*, a voice screamed inside him. *You're letting it get all complicated again.*

As if he had a choice?

As if he'd had a choice from the first moment he'd seen her?

They reached the top and Kylie's hands went to the bottom of his sweatshirt. She tugged it and the cotton shirt underneath it up to his chest, lingering her fingers there as Mac felt the cool air spill across his belly, felt himself breathing it in and out.

Her fingers tightened and bunched, demanding he raise his arms.

~~~~

*I've been able to stand on my own two feet since I was one,* she'd told him when they'd met. And she'd been like that with everything. Her schooling, her job, her men. No one had ever helped her or handed anything to her. She'd had to work for it and *demand* it to make it hers.

Except in sex. As if she'd always been afraid she wasn't good enough, attractive enough, sexy enough. So she'd never demanded like this, like she felt compelled to do with Macaulay. The power he gave her was intoxicating.

As he raised his arms she slid his sweatshirt, and the shirt under it, up and over his head. He shrugged it off and stood there for her while she ran her hands lightly over the muscle and curly hair. Then her hands dropped to his ski pants and pulled them down and off.

~~~~

It was all Mac could do to keep himself from grabbing Kylie's hands, stopping her and taking control. But he sensed deep in his gut that she needed this, needed the control, at least at first.

When she'd pulled his pants and jockey shorts all the way down, he stepped out of them and let her run her fingers slowly up his legs and sides. His erection rose with them. He watched her see it, take it in with her eyes, then look up to his face.

She smiled, her fingers playing lightly around the sides of his chest.

"My turn," he said dryly.

A quick flicker of fear shot through her eyes but then she nodded and stepped back ever so slightly to give him access.

With excruciating control, his naked body quivering, he reached for the bottom of her turtleneck. He held her eyes as he drew it up and, when she raised her arms, over her head. Her hair tumbled like curls of silk to her shoulders and he had to look.

The skin of her shoulders, her neck, her upper breasts shone in the indirect light like soft porcelain. The straps and cups of her flesh-colored bra seemed grossly cheap by comparison. So he thoughtfully removed them.

Her nipples popped out, swollen pink and proud. He let his fingers trace around them once, his hands take the weight of her breasts, feel their fullness and heat.

"Macaulay, hurry," she whispered, and his control was gone.

~~~~

What kind of lawyer must he have been, Kylie gasped inside, as Macaulay grabbed her and pulled her to the bed. One minute he was impossibly controlled; the next, a wild animal.

He pushed her down and tugged off her ski pants, long underwear, and panties, all at once.

When they caught around her toes, she frantically kicked them.

Then he was on her, their naked flesh meeting in a thump, and their bodies began to thrash together like out-of-control teens. His arms pulled her against him, squeezing her buttocks, running up and down her back, fingers wrapping through her hair. He pulled her head back to ravish her mouth with his again and again.

And she was on him too. Her fingers dug hard into his arms as her legs wrapped around his center and squeezed him like he was a log in a torrent she had to cling to for dear life. She was under him. On top of him. Rolling.

His scent! A hot animal smell that mingled with the perfume of the sheets and somehow the smell of the forest outside. The sweat of his kisses. The sound of their skin brushing skin. It was like she was being turned inside out. Some hunger he'd tapped in her was bursting forth, threatening to spill out in crazy sobs.

Then he rolled her under him and pressed himself up from her to look into her face.

He was breathing hard, flushed. She could feel the throbbing erection of him on her left leg. His eyes were dark and fierce, but there was nothing hidden in them. His whole being was want, written there, looking down at her, her completely.

"Can I come in?" he said.

It was so foolish that they both twitched smiles together. And dropped them.

"Oh, God, yes, but..."

He held up a condom he'd pulled from somewhere and rolled it on.

Kylie spread wide for him in invitation.

He nodded and dropped his head down quickly to her breasts, his teeth finding first one nipple, then the other, nibbling lightly so that shots of electric fire shot straight to her groin and made her flood. Made her ache to be filled.

She was about to say this, or scream at him to enter her or leave and never come back, when he drew up his head, reached down, and guided himself in.

The flood of sensation carried her legs up unconsciously to wrap around him again, pull him down to her like she could somehow absorb this torrential power that was beating into her very center, driving her into a rhythm so primal that she lost track of where she ended and he began.

They were beating at each other, riding each other, lost in each other. Higher and higher, up and down in waves and crests, until finally one wave was ridden so high that, as he reached down and touched her in the chaos, it spilled over inside and burst like an bomb. Her muscles clenched, top to bottom, and shook like she'd stuck her finger in a light socket. Exploding ripples over and over. On and on. So she cried out in a high whimper a part of her remembered from somewhere, some long forgotten truth of herself.

Herself. Her real self. This.

Finally, after a trembling pause, her body understood it was done and threw itself back in exhaustion.

Only to be pulled back from there with the power of Macaulay driving himself to his own climax. And the power of that, of his throaty gasping, the almost-frightening strength of his contraction, made Kylie curl up around him one more time and share the electricity as she could not remember sharing anything so intensely in her life.

~~~~

When it was done, when all the gasping and final convulsions had stopped, when they'd both collapsed, exhausted, side-by-side, still entwined, Mac smoothed some wildly twisted hair out of Kylie's eyes and gazed into them in wonderment.

"What?" she said and laughed, a bubbling, free sound.

"You," he said.

"What about me?"

"Just..." He paused for a second, examining his impulse to just spill to her rather than weigh and carefully analyze the effect of every word. Maybe he was in a new life after all. "When I first saw you in that impossibly form-fitting red ski outfit..."

"Bolger. Their latest line. I was the one who picked them out for our Seattle store."

"Uh-hunh," said Mac, smiling. "Exactly. I saw you in a suit you'd carefully picked out, with your hair all made up, your makeup all snooty perfect, the attitude to match..."

"I was not snooty."

"...the idea of ending up in this sort of position with you was, shall we say, kind of low on the scale of possibilities."

"It *was* low on the scale," Kylie said. "Just about off the bottom of the scale."

"And it got even lower later. At my apartment."

Kylie propped herself up on one elbow. Mac liked the way that made her breasts tumble sideways and was about to comment when he saw how serious she'd suddenly become.

"The thing is," she said slowly, her eyes studying the sheets between them, "I have a thing about quitting. I've had to pretty much make my own life. I left home early. I worked my way through university, got every job I've had by myself. My parents... All they wanted me to be when I grew up was a housewife. Actually, strike that. I'm not sure they even thought about me that much. I was supposed to be a boy, and when they didn't get that, they pretty much just wrote me off."

Mac started to say something, but she shook her head.

"It wasn't like they were mean," she said. "They took care of me when I was young, bought me clothes, and toys, sent me to riding classes, karate classes, art classes. But when I saw how they treated Sam— Actually, that's not fair. Even Samantha only got half their attention. They were—*are*—just not very good at caring about anyone outside of themselves."

She looked up finally and caught his eyes. "So the idea of giving up law, where you have so much power to help people and make something of yourself, to bum around as a snowboard instructor... I don't get that."

She waited, obviously inviting him to speak.

And Mac stared back, his lips tight. After all this, how could he make her understand? However wild she might be in bed, she was at heart a control freak. Even this thing of trying to save her sister, that was probably some weird sibling rivalry thing somehow. Or proving something to her parents?

How did you explain to someone like that the case he'd fought for Melanie Carson? The sort of injustice that was the final straw, that made him need to walk away from it all?

Like Kylie had just said: she had a thing about quitting.

"I guess," he said finally, "that I took on one desperate case too many. And when I wasn't good enough for it, I figured maybe I'd better leave the practice of law to people who were."

She looked at him in confusion, maybe a little bit hurt? "Can you explain that a little? Tell me about the case?"

"No." Mac rolled up out of bed, feeling the chill of the suite rush around his body. "I don't think I can."

He grabbed his pants, underwear, and top, and went down the stairs.

Kylie joined him a few minutes later, but she too seemed to have realized that their little frenzy upstairs had been a mistake. Without asking him to join her, she unwrapped the chocolates and sampled a few, along with half the strawberries. She fiddled with the gas fireplace until she got it going. Then she called the concierge and asked him to bring his and hers toilet kits to the suite.

Mac almost turned to her twice when he thought he caught her looking at him. Maybe he could...

But no. He had to be realistic. Come on. Whatever he might feel for her, he understood at last why she could never feel the same towards him. His failure had messed up his life three years ago. He was broken and there was no quick fix. No easy out. Certainly not with Kylie Michaelson who needed a whole man, not one like him.

Just before bed—Kylie had brushed her teeth with a

toothbrush from the delivered toilet kits and Mac had made it clear he'd sleep on the couch downstairs—Kylie said, "Do you at least have an idea to rescue Samantha?"

He looked up at her where she stood on the stairs. "I'll talk to my brother tomorrow. He works with Tibor. Maybe there's something he can do."

"But what about you? Don't you work with Tibor? Or for Tibor?"

He looked away from her. "I never said that."

"Yes, you did. You said you work for the Balakirevs."

"Balakirev singular." He grabbed the second toothbrush from the toilet kits and headed for the washroom. "I'm doing a job for Leonid, Tibor's father."

# 12

KYLIE LAY IN THE WIDE BED with her mind whirring. She'd lain down almost two hours ago but hadn't been able to sleep. The sounds of Macaulay preparing to sleep drifted up over the railing to her. Her mind's eye watched him strip down to his underwear and throw that extra pillow they'd found onto one of the too-short love seats. He'd pick up the extra blanket that had been with the pillow, and lay his body down...

Argh. Kylie pulled her own pillow around her head.

There was so much of Macaulay that was a mystery to her. On the one hand he had this incredible male competence about him. He almost reeked it. It overpowered her whenever she got too close to him. She'd seen it in the way he manipulated Tibor Balakirev and casually controlled the hulking Maksim.

On the other, he kept running away from things, from his job, from his ability to help, from Kylie herself. How could he drop a bombshell like the fact he was doing "a job" for Leonid Balakirev and refuse to say more? Didn't he see that all he had to do was tell her something, anything, to explain himself, and she was his in an instant?

She squirmed and rolled over in bed, smelling the scent of him still there. Remembering the power of his arms and legs, the completeness of him inside her.

Even without an explanation, she was probably his. Just a simple touch...

Ah, yes, she thought cynically and flung herself flat on her back again, staring at the ceiling. The renowned Michaelson smart choices in men. Who cares what they're like on the inside, so long as they're good in bed and look like gods in a business suit or on the ski slope.

What *did* Macaulay look like in a suit?

And the way he'd so patiently been instructing those teens, the way he'd stepped in to help find Samantha even after she'd rebuffed him—how could a man be so adamant about not caring and so obviously care?

A creak of springs from the main room below grabbed her attention.

She could hear the gentle hiss of the gas fireplace, she realized. The howling blizzard outside had subsided to a quiet snowfall.

Muted beeps from below. Macaulay was calling someone on his cell phone.

Sliding ever so slowly from her sheets, she managed to leave the bed without a sound. She crept to the edge of the loft and peered over its waist-high wall.

Macaulay was sitting on the edge of the second love seat, the bare muscles of his bare back to her, his head bowed over as he held the cell phone to his ear. And though he was whispering, Kylie could make out most of it.

"Yes, I've got her right here...I don't know...She's convinced her sister was at the party...Yes...Yes, I agree...What do you want me to do?"

Kylie felt cold slush slide through her veins. Yes, Macaulay was a mystery, but he was now becoming a frightening one.

As she watched him unconsciously nod over his instructions on the phone, Kylie stepped cautiously back from the edge wall of the loft.

Who was he speaking with? Leonid Balakirev? Or was it really Tibor? Could Kylie trust that anything he'd told her about his dealings with them was true?

"Okay," she heard him say. "Tomorrow." There was a quiet shut-down melody. The cell phone conversation was over.

So was her trust in Macaulay.

Kylie crept back into bed with a sick feeling in the pit of her stomach. It was another hour before she finally slept.

# 13

THEY'RE GONE."

"Wha—?"

Kylie reeled back to consciousness to find Macaulay fully dressed in his clothes from yesterday, staring down at her from beside her bed in the loft.

She grabbed the sheet and blanket to cover herself, feeling foolish as she did. But she saw his nostrils flare and eyes dart over the still-exposed side of her, the bare leg and panties, the side of her tee-shirt-clad torso. Her bra, she remembered was somewhere over by the wall where Macaulay had tossed it last night.

She blinked and Macaulay's eyes were hard, his mouth set in a rigidly neutral line. Right. She herself, she remembered, was no longer interested in him either.

"Who's gone?" she asked finally.

"Your sister, if she was ever here. Tibor. My brother, John. Alyssa. All the Japanese and their dates."

"How...?"

"I was up two hours ago. I went to find John. The central registry in the lodge tracks where every guest at the resort is staying. He was registered at the Hillside but he checked out early this morning. I presume he left, since the snowplows cleared the roads by seven. The others were all gone too—Tibor, his stable of six women who were are all listed simply as his 'guests,' and the Japanese investors, all listed under the name Hachiuma Sato."

"Sato? The guy you came down with?"

"That's right. Maybe their CEO, president, something. Maybe just a designated name man." He looked pointedly towards the half wall and the sliver of window she could see from her place on the bed. Bright sunshine lit the entire suite. The snow had stopped.

"I guess I overslept," she said, stretching and unable to stop herself from letting her sheet slip a little bit as she watched his face.

"I guess you did," he said coldly. He looked only at her face and she again felt foolish.

"So what now?" she said.

"Now we get up, get dressed, and leave. Tibor only loaned us this suite for the night."

"I mean after that." Kylie hated this. Her throat was closing up. It felt like a high school break up. What was with her anyway? It wasn't the first time a man had let her down.

Macaulay turned from her and walked to the top of the stairs. "After that, I guess you can do what you like. Stay here, keep asking around about your sister. Whatever. I suspect she's long gone now, though. Tibor's finished with her. He's probably turned her loose. She might be on her way back home across the border."

"You believe that?"

His hand tapped the half-wall that separated the loft from

the main room below. He didn't turn to look at her as he spoke. "I don't know. I'm catching the bus back to Vancouver in twenty minutes. I've got a class to teach there on Grouse Mountain."

"So that's it?"

He paused. "Yup."

"No final advice? Nothing?"

He paused so long this time she thought he was just going to stalk down the stairs and out. When he did speak, his voice was like flesh over gravel. "Sometimes, Kylie, you take on more than you should. Your sister, I'm sure, is going to be fine. This adventure is over. Go home. Let her find her own way home. Sometimes that's the best thing you can do for people."

He waited.

"Will you go?" he demanded, still not looking at her.

"I..." Why did it feel like her insides were becoming all unglued? "I...yes."

He nodded once, then he did leave. Without another word or look.

Kylie threw herself on the bed and sobbed.

~~~~

Stomping away from the Creekside, Mac shook his head repeatedly, swearing under his breath.

That woman! Why, no matter how foolish his head said she was, or how little he had to offer her, did his heart still race like mad when he was around her? The memory of her touch was too strong, of her panting, the way her skin slid and tensed under his hands, her little cries.

Which was just lust, right? So why was he doing what he

was doing now? Ignoring his orders to stay close to her so they could keep track of her, and instead sending her away. Sending her home. While he stupidly picked up her investigation for her.

Did he believe that Tibor was just going to let Samantha go once the Japanese he'd assigned her to was done?

Not on your life. If Tibor was drugging these girls, as Mac suspected, he'd already crossed way over the casual use or favor line. He'd bought and paid for them. And if there was one thing Mac knew about Tibor from all his dealings with him over the years, it was that Tibor rarely gave up things he'd bought and paid for.

Mac reached the Lodge, retrieved his snowboard and helmet, and wandered down to the edge of the parking lot where the morning bus was due to stop by in just a few minutes. A small line of skiers and snowboards, probably trapped here as he had been yesterday, were lined up on one side of the snow bank, a few with faces flush from a quick, early morning run. The lifts had only started running twenty minutes ago.

Mac hadn't totally lied to Kylie. He *was* going to catch the bus back to Vancouver. But he wasn't going back to teach snowboarding. He'd taken a sabbatical from all his Grouse and Cypress teaching when he'd gotten Tibor to give him the classes at Milaya Ridge. No, what Mac had planned was a little face-to-face with John and with Leonid. One of them certainly knew more than they were saying. One of them certainly had to have the pull to change things.

And again he wondered why he was doing it. If prickly-but-delectable Kylie wasn't even going to be here anymore, what was his payoff?

A good deed? A reflexive raging against injustice?

The bus arrived and stopped at the head of the line with a grind of brakes and a hiss of hydraulics as the front doors released. Mac joined the others in sticking his snowboard into the exterior carry racks.

Maybe, he thought as he showed his pass and climbed aboard, it was just a vague outside shot at recovering what it was he'd lost with the Melanie Carson case. Self-confidence. Integrity. Hope.

He took a seat and grimaced out the frosted window. Like he'd told Kylie back in that loft where he'd momentarily felt like he'd found some kind of salvation—sometimes people had to find their own way home.

Which, in his case, meant him helping someone who couldn't. The irony wasn't lost on him.

~~~~

He'd lied to her, so Kylie had lied to him. It was that simple, she told herself uneasily as she approached one of the clerks in the reception area of the lodge.

Besides, if he truly understood her, he'd have known she could never leave until she was sure her sister was safe.

Kylie set down her bound together skis, boots, and poles—the cheap binding straps had been provided by the sweet concierge at the Creekside—and asked the young girl at the counter if there truly was a central registry for all the guests who were visiting the Milaya Ridge resort.

"Um...yes, there is, ma'am. But it's just for management."

"Really." Kylie let her face fall. How had Macaulay seen it then? Or had that been a lie? "It's just...I'm looking for my sister, to see if she actually got checked in her last night."

"Oh. Oh, well," said the girl, who couldn't have been more than eighteen and was as tanned as Macaulay and Bo and all the other ski/board bunnies running around up here. "What's your name?"

She gave it and the girl's face lit up. "I have a note for you! Two!"

She pulled them out of a slot somewhere under the desk and handed them over. Kylie unfolded the first, read Bo's repeated apology about abandoning her on the slopes last night—it already felt like another lifetime after what had happened afterwards—and asking to meet her for breakfast or lunch.

Kylie crumpled it and tossed it into the corner trash can. *That* wasn't going to happen.

When she opened the second note, her eyes went so wide that the girl behind the counter leaned forward, trying to see. "What is it?" she asked.

"It's from my baby sister," Kylie whispered, her fingers making the paper shake as she read the hurried scrawl.

*Kylie*, it said. *Saw you. Heard you. Help. S.*

~~~~

"You should have just made the big sister vanish on the hills when you had the chance," the partner said. "The storm was a perfect cover."

"Yes, well," Tibor said. He eyed his guests and their escorts as they laughed and pointed their ways through the softly-lit, enclosed spaces of the Vancouver Aquarium. This had been Jun Maruyama's choice. He was an avid collector of exotic fish. Tibor wondered idly if he or one of his cohorts would stoop to trying to steal or buy some of the more unusual species they saw here this morning. "Sometimes the people we hire to do a job let us down. Then we make backup plans."

"To kill her?"

Tibor shook back his hair and observed the partner coolly. "If that becomes necessary. But it would be such a waste. She is not unattractive and she comes from such a good family. Have you noticed?"

He gestured to a darker alcove along the viewing room to the right. There, separated from the rest of the group, but doing little to conceal their activities, the bug-eyed Japanese named Ogano Takahashi (or Takahashi Ogano, if you put the surname first according to their custom) was pawing at his escort, the challenging Samantha Michaelson.

Even under the regular supply-and-withhold schedule of crystal meth that bound all Tibor's girls to him, Samantha Michaelson had struggled repeatedly to break herself free. She'd tried to steal Tibor's cell phone. She'd privately begged Ogano to "rescue" her.

Ogano had talked to Tibor about it. Plans were made.

"What are you thinking?" the partner demanded.

"Just this," said Tibor. "Sometimes the visitors to a stable want to buy a horse. If you must sell, how fortunate you must be to have another from the same family to replace your loss."

"You can pull that off? Both the sale and another kidnap?"

Tibor turned to her with a cruel smile. "You still don't see what you have grown up with. This is North America. Here you can do anything."

# 14

JEEZ. He couldn't find John. Couldn't find Tibor. Mac was really batting a thousand so far.

"Mr. Rush?" said Leonid's heavy-set secretary, Kathy. "Mr. Balakirev will see you now."

Mac popped up off the cracked leather couches in the waiting room and strode to the door. He'd gone home first, ditched his snowboard and gear and changed into some upscale casual clothes. Though he wondered, as he pushed through the door and Leonid waved him into the smoke-filled office, why he'd bothered.

Leonid Balakirev, sixty-eight years old and built like his Brezhnev namesake, Russian square, thick eyebrows over pouchy eyes and a long lower face, was hardly one to be impressed by appearances. He ran his multi-million dollar cargo shipping business out of one of the many concrete eyesores along Jasmine Road, right by the waterfront. When Mac pushed in through his office door, he had to wave a hand in front of his face. The walls were grimy, the gray carpet so scuffed and burned it would have looked good on a factory floor, and the air was the same color as both, choked with unfiltered cigarette smoke.

Mac grimaced and waved his hand in front of his face. "Still trying to fumigate, I see."

"The advantages of owning your own shipping containers," Leonid said in his thick accent and waved his burning cigarette around. "The very strongest cigarettes money can buy."

"Why not roll your own. No filter."

"Too much work. Too much work. Can I offer you one? No? Vodka? Alright." He stubbed out his cigarette in a full ashtray and turned to close the blinds behind him. When he turned back, his heavy face looked dark as mud. "Talk to me, my friend. Why are you being so stupid?"

Mac felt the threat but wasn't buying. For some reason, knowing that Kylie was safe and it was just him made him feel lighter than any time since Alyssa walked out on him.

"Tibor's messing up big time, Leo."

Leonid blew out dismissively. "Of course. It is why I asked you to keep an eye on him for me."

"These girls he's using to persuade his new investors—I figure he's got them all hooked on something. That means he's probably into the drug trade now."

Leonid shook his head. It looked like a jowly dog shaking off a flea. "Everyone is in the drug trade in this city. How could you not be in the drug trade here?"

"You?"

"Except me, of course."

"I mean it," Mac said tightly. "Are you dealing in drugs? Shipping them? Laundering money? Any of those?"

Leonid glowered at him, his heavy brows down, his face in shadow. Then he walked around his desk slowly toward Mac, seeming to grow in bulk until he stopped less than a foot from

Mac. "Macaulay Rush." He drew the words out heavily. "We have known each other for how many years now? Ten? Twelve? And you ask me this?"

"I ask you this."

Leonid placed a large porkchop of a hand on Mac's shoulder and looked into his eyes. "The second hardest thing I have ever done is fight off the people who have tried to take my business into the darkness. This is why I called on you for help with the hardest thing. With my son. You understand the cost of this fight."

Mac narrowed his eyes to look into the older man's and saw the deep sense of integrity confirmed. He'd gut-level known this before but had needed to be sure. It was why only Leonid would understand what Mac was about to tell him now.

~~~~

Kylie pulled her rented Grand Am to a stop in the gravel lot of Leonid Balakirev's offices. Near the door, a black motorbike gleamed in the sun. A matching black helmet was clipped casually onto its handlebar as if no one would dare steal it in this lot, this place.

Kylie stared at it as she climbed out in her skirt and high heels. *Danger*, it chirped for some reason. She again had that tingly feeling up the back of her neck that she was being watched.

But she didn't have a choice. After reading Sam's note and sharing it with the clerk, the clerk had broken down and let her see the resort log books. They confirmed everything Macaulay had told her. Tibor was out. The six Japanese and their "guests" were out. John and Alyssa Rush had checked out early.

It had left Leonid Balakirev as her only solid lead. On a

hunch, she'd changed into her sexiest professional attire before coming to meet him this time. Asking politely hadn't gotten her an audience last time. This time she was going to try sex and chutzpah, not necessarily in that order.

The first test came as soon as she'd wobbled up to the front door. There was the same security guard who'd turned her away before. This time she strode in without even looking at him and dashed up one flight of stairs to where she figured the older Balakirev kept his offices.

The first one she ducked into had two large desks, endless file cabinets, and stank of cigarettes. The two tie-and-shirt-sleeve drones looked up from their papers in consternation, cancer sticks dangling from their mouths.

Before they could say anything, Kylie heard the guard from downstairs pound up the stairwell. Kylie made a pleading face at the two workers and stepped behind the open door, a filing cabinet at her back.

She heard the guard in stick his head, ask something in Russian and get non-emotional replies. Then the guard was gone. Kylie waited a moment, slid out, and beamed at the two men. They looked at each other then smiled broadly at her.

The first butted out his cigarette, slicked back his choppy hair and said, "You mistress, yes?"

"Pardon?" said Kylie.

"Mr. Balakirev," the second said. The cigarette jiggled between his lips as he spoke and spilled ash on the table. "He wife, Duscha, here all the time. She think she know."

"Ah," said Kylie, licking her lips and sticking out some pantyhosed bare leg in a way she hoped wasn't *too* obvious. "That's right. Mr. Balakirev and me. Could you, maybe, check to make sure that guard is gone?"

The one with the choppy hair jumped from his seat and walked to the door, looked out both directions. "He gone."

"And, um, could you just check that his wife isn't in Mr. Balakirev's offices?"

"She not come in today," said the second guy, still at his desk.

Kylie reached out a hand and touched the choppy head's cheek. "Could you just check anyway?"

He smiled hugely—some dental work needed there—and walked quickly down the hall with Kylie following, turned the corner, held up a hand, and opened a door. He stuck his head in, asked something in Russian, got a response, and pulled his head out again.

"She not come in today."

"Thank you so much," Kylie cooed. She leaned in and kissed him on the cheek. It left a large red lipstick mark and Kylie pulled out a facial tissue from her purse to wipe it off. Choppy head stopped her.

"No. No. I show," he said, and trotted happily back the way he had come.

Her spirits brighter, Kylie straightened her hair, entered Balakirev's outer office, and fought hard to keep her judgement of the poor decor and cigarette smell here too, off her face. The overweight secretary/receptionist who for some reason reminded Kylie of Kylie's granny, if her granny had been thirty years younger, slid her glasses down her nose and looked Kylie up and down, unimpressed. "What can I do for you, hon?"

Kylie assumed her best confident-buyer stance. "I'm here to see Mr. Balakirev."

"For what?"

Kylie debated the mistress ploy but decided the woman would see through it. "Business," she said.

"Not likely," said the guardian. "You're hardly the shipping type, and he only sees people here by appointment." She waved her hand pointedly around the room. "Not exactly a drop-in kind of place."

Kylie ransacked her brain for a creative lie, but that had never been her strong suit. "Okay, look," she said finally. "I'm looking for my sister and there's a good chance she's tied up with Mr. Balakirev's son, Tibor. Maybe against her will. It's my fault she's up here and it's my job to rescue her, so if you could just..." Surprisingly she found her eyes had grown wet.

Just as surprisingly, the hard face of the secretary softened too. "Ahem. Not sure Mr. Balakirev can do anything to help you, hon."

"Maybe not. Maybe." Kylie sniffed and reached into her purse. She pulled out Samantha's picture, and showed it. "Does she look familiar?"

"Hm. Pretty. Younger sister?"

Kylie nodded.

"You very close?"

"Once upon a time. Again. My fault." She had to quickly dig for the tissue she'd offered choppy head. What was with her all of a sudden?

"It's okay, hon. Really." The big woman eased herself back from her desk and indicated a red light on her intercom phone. "You know, just maybe Mr. B. could talk to you when he's done his present meeting. But just remember he doesn't see his son much these days. They had a bit of a falling out, if you know what I mean."

Kylie finished dabbing her eyes and nose and tucked away her tissue. "But...isn't Mr. Balakirev part of the financing for Milaya Ridge?"

"Milaya Ridge?" The secretary laughed and her eyes sparkled. "Honey, that place is such a money sinkhole and legislative mess. Mr. B. warned Tibor away from that, but Mr. B.'s lawyer, see, caught a bit of Tibor's needing to prove himself better than daddy."

"This...lawyer sold Tibor on it?"

"Hook, line, and sinker. Emphasis on the sinker part. I'm betting Tibor's been doing anything he can to raise money ever since."

"And the lawyer?" Kylie pressed.

"Rush. That's his name. Appropriate, hunh."

"Does he still work for Mr. Balakirev senior?"

"Oh, occasionally. In fact..."

She cut it off as the inner door to Balakirev's office suddenly opened, releasing a billowing smell of cigarette smoke that almost made Kylie gag. The gagging reflex turned to shock as she saw an older man walk out, thickset and heavy-browed, with his arm slung around Macaulay Rush's shoulders like he was a favorite uncle.

Both men stopped when they saw Kylie.

"Macaulay," she blurted.

The older man smiled. It made the pouches under his eyes bag outwards so he looked like some monstrous toad. Hard to believe he'd fathered the hawk-nosed, svelte Tibor. "This must be the girl you told me about, yes?" he said in an accent as thick as that of his shirt-sleeve workers down the hall. "The one you want to help."

Help how? Kylie wondered bitterly. "Did you—?" she began.

Macaulay stepped out from Balakirev's arm and grabbed Kylie's. "I think we'd better talk about it outside," he said and began walking her that way.

Kylie tore herself free. "No. I came here to speak to Mr. Balakirev."

"Then I shall walk out with both of you," said the older man. "Come!"

Before she could protest, the Leonid Balakirev somehow had his arm linked with her and was gliding her down the hall in a graceful dance. So his parentage of Tibor might be believable after all.

"Macaulay used to be your lawyer?" she asked as they passed the room of the shirt-sleeved guys. Choppy head grinned and gave her a thumbs up.

"I had a car accident. I had workers getting hurt. Yes. Mac was the best at his job, so I hired him."

"Mac. And he still works for you?" They descended the stairs. Macaulay was walking quietly behind.

"Not as a lawyer," Balakirev said.

They were out in the lot now and Balakirev walked straight to the black motorcycle. He ran a hand over its fuel tank and looked back at Macaulay. "You bought it."

"I did," Macaulay said, suddenly right beside her, arm to arm. "A divorce present to myself. Three years later."

"I like it," Balakirev said.

"I don't," Kylie said. She didn't like what it said about Macaulay, *Mac*, about this rebellious side of him that was filled with danger and secrets. And that chill feeling had crept up the back of her neck again. A motor revved somewhere.

Macaulay stepped back from her, giving her space, and suddenly the motor she'd heard revved high and tires squealed. Kylie looked to her left to see an old blue pickup truck, its driver wearing a ski mask, heading straight for her!

# 15

Mac's eyes shot to Leonid, thinking he was the target, then saw the trajectories were wrong and ran for Kylie, tackling her out of the way against an old Chevy Corsica.

He rolled off her and turned. The truck had skidded in a turning, banging off two other parked cars and was lining up with Kylie again.

*Crack!*

A firecracker sounded and a chip flew from the truck.

No! It was a gunshot. Leonid, the old action hero, had pulled a gun out of somewhere on his person and was aiming for a second shot at the truck's driver.

This was obviously beyond the driver's scope of service because he cranked the wheel hard left and took off across the lot, losing track of where the exit was. Leonid tracked him, his large nostrils flaring and face red.

The truck was skid-turning a second time, this time lining up for the exit.

Without thinking beyond the need to end the threat, Mac dashed for his motorbike, ripped the helmet from the handlebars, and yanked it onto his head even as he swung a leg over. A second later he jumped on the kick-start and tore up the dirt as he roared after the truck.

He thought he saw Kylie running for her car as he leapt the bumpy entrance of the lot in a cloud of dust and skidded onto Jasmine Road. But he didn't have time to check. The truck was heading west, straight towards the downtown.

If he'd headed east, towards the Second Narrows, towards the highway, the arteries choked up with just enough space on the side he could have ridden him down like a cowboy. But the truck was roaring onto the wide one-ways heading downtown, maybe hoping to shake pursuit on one of the hundred side streets.

Mac spat the grit of Leonid's parking lot from his mouth and sped after it.

~~~~

What was he doing? What was he *doing!?*

And what was *she* doing, Kylie thought as she slammed the door of her Grand Am and gunned the engine, skidding out of the lot just a few second behind Mac.

The pickup truck driver—he'd tried to kill her! And Macaulay had saved her, Balakirev had pulled a gun, Mac had jumped on his motorcycle...

Up ahead she saw Mac leaning hard left to follow the truck onto that broad street she'd followed to get her. A one way. Good. She could at least know which direction—

An SUV blared its horn at her as she skidded onto the one-way in front of it. Then she was leaping forward again, her foot pressed to the pedal.

This isn't a race car, her rational mind kept saying. This isn't TV. But her adrenaline was pumping so furiously now that the thought barely registered. She had to know what happened. Had to be there. She would not be left out! And it was all she could do to swerve around the traffic and safely fly through the red lights with her foot flooring the accelerator.

They'd turned!

They were whipping down a street to the right, and a shambling man and woman who looked like they'd stumbled out of a bad skid row film were crossing the street where she had to follow.

Swearing loudly, she shot by the turn and headed for the next, hoping to catch them there or snag a police escort or something. But there were never police to catch you speeding when you *needed* one.

At the next street, she skidded right, ignoring the honks and shouts and tore down the road only to see the pickup truck and Mac still hot on its tail whip by in front of her.

She wheeled madly left in pursuit.

Cobblestone streets, jumping pedestrians, pavement again, honking cars and squealing brakes. Kylie herself kept stomping on the brakes to slow and swerve around sudden traffic and people. Until her inner voice was screaming loud enough to be heard now.

*Crazy! Lunatic! You'll kill yourself, or worse, someone else! You'll kill a kid!*

Except she was trying to *rescue* a kid too. Her baby sister. This guy in the pickup—he had to know where she was or he'd never had attacked Kylie. And Mac was chasing him. Mac had to know what he was doing.

Mac. *Mac.* So much easier. Simpler. Just a guy...

A guy leaning back and forth on his motorbike ahead of her like he was Wild Bill!

Kylie gulped as she floored the gas pedal and managed to shoot between two cars ahead of her, gaining almost a car length in the pursuit.

Then suddenly, she wasn't sure how, they were on the long entrance to Stanley Park, thick with traffic roaring through the center, the pickup turning at the last minute to take the one-way peel-off lanes that led around the slow shoreline.

Kylie swerved around the Audi in front of her, scared two inline skaters wobbling along the sidewalk nearby, and tore after them.

A boat club flew by on her right. Joggers, cyclists, inline skaters, walkers, a horse-drawn carriage, trees, water. Everything came in flashes as she tried to keep up without hitting anything. Her mouth was dry as toast, tasted like paste, her face clammy and wet, hair in clumps beside it. Her fingers and legs ached from the stress of clenching.

Then, as she slowed slightly to swerve up a narrow, winding road that climbed away from the water, into the trees, her nightmare blossomed before her.

The pickup truck, maybe thirty yards ahead around the curve, must have done a skid left to block the road. Because he was suddenly there, sideways, and Mac was laying down his own bike to skid before impact.

Kylie slammed on her own brakes, standing on the pedal so hard she rose off her seat.

The Grand Am screamed and skidded, slewed sideways, she steered into the skid and corrected, it jerked the other way, Mac and his bike hit the side of the pickup with a grinding crash, the

Grand Am fishtailed once more...and stopped.

"Mac!" Kylie screamed and flung open her door, leaping out and running.

Suddenly there was a grinding sound and the pickup truck spun its rear wheels and lurched forward at an angle, its right tires cranked hard right.

It drove *over* the front tire of Macaulay's motorcycle that had become wedged under its middle. In the popping, cracking sound of it, Kylie imagined Mac's legs going and almost dropped in cold faint, but didn't. She ran up just as Mac pulling himself rapidly back from the wreckage, apparently unharmed.

"Sonofa..." she heard him grunt. Then he pulled himself up to his feet, stumbling a little and clutching his left side.

The pickup wheeled blithely onto what Kylie saw was a merge lane that suddenly opened in the trees to join this roundabout park road to the four-lane roadway that ran through its center. In the rear window, she saw the masked driver hold up a hand and flip them a finger.

Mac grunted again and she ran to steady him.

As her head popped up under his arm, he looked down with honest shock on his face. "Kylie? How...?"

"Never mind. We need to move your bike off the road. And my car. You have a cell?"

He snorted and pulled it from a belt holder. "If it's not broken."

But when he flipped it open and keyed it on, the signal came in strong. Ten minutes later the tow truck and police arrived.

It was a good hour and a half after that when the Vancouver Police finished questioning them, with a warning that charges could be laid and they weren't to leave the area, and let them drive off in the rented Grand Am.

~~~~

"My place or yours," Kylie said when they finally managed to get turned around to head back into the downtown core.

Macaulay, scraped, bruised, and wasp angry over the condition of his motorcycle, wiped his face with both hands. "Mine, if that's okay," he said. "Need to change. And we need to do some honest planning now."

Kylie nodded. Mac's left pant leg, some kind of synthetic ski pant that she suspected he mostly lived in these days, had been shredded when he'd laid down his bike to avoid hitting head on. The medics who'd arrived with the fire truck had cut it away and cleaned and bandaged the skin, recommending he have it checked in the next day or so.

Kylie herself smelled stale. The odor of the chase, the sweat, the pasty-mouth taste, still lingered. Her hair felt limp and tangled. And while vanity seemed foolish just then, she longed to have a good mirror, maybe even a shower.

"Do you have something else I could wear at your place?"

Mac shot her a wary glance. "I guess." The glance flicked quickly down to her bare legs, Kylie noted.

"Okay, then."

Fifteen minutes later, with minimal direction from Macaulay, Kylie pulled into the same visitor's spot at the top of the wharf where she'd parked last time. Feels a little like coming home, she thought, and then had to scramble out of the car because the thought unnerved her.

Unlike the day before when she'd been here, the sky was a breathtaking blue today, like the snowstorm had purged something from the air. The sun glittered off the water of False Creek. Beautiful. Twice as beautiful because she and Mac had just come close to death and hadn't died. It made every lungful of air sweet and full, its smell a delight.

"You're going to have to help me down the ramp," Kylie said.

"What?"

"My shoes. High heels."

He looked, his eyes lingering on her legs again. That was *not* a ploy on her part, Kylie insisted to herself. Though, if there was one part of her body she'd always been able to count on, it was her legs. Her exercise regimen had always included lots of Stairmaster.

Mac tore his eyes away and nodded. When they reached the top of the metal ramp leading down, he offered her his arm. She took it, leaning in close. He walked stolidly down beside her as if he didn't notice.

Stop that, she scolded herself again. As he limped a little at the bottom, she was doubly mortified.

"Oh, my gosh," she said. "I'm so sorry. Your leg. I forgot."

"It's not that bad." But he winced again as they made it to his door and in.

"Can I help you get your bath?" He raised an eyebrow at her and she blushed. "I mean get up to it? Climb the stairs. Long as I don't have to wear these." She kicked off her shoes and dropped her purse beside it.

He smiled now and shook his head. "Just give me about fifteen minutes. Have a seat. Look around. Down here."

She felt another flush of embarrassment. The unspoken dis-invitation to go upstairs again told her as clearly as a growl that he hadn't forgotten her last visit here. He'd revealed a bit of himself upstairs, in his bedroom and office, only to have her throw it back in his face.

In fact, she remembered as he limped up the stairs, she'd pretty much accused him of being part of Tibor's prostitution ring. And whether she'd said it or not—she couldn't remember now how many stupid things she'd said—she'd decided he was a failure. He'd run from his career. He'd lost his wife to his younger brother. He'd become a lowly snowboard instructor in the employ of the Balakirevs.

Yet what was she *supposed* to think?

She began padding around his living room, idly fingering his books and knick-knacks. They were all simple, as she'd noted before, but not as bland as she'd thought at first. They held a strong Aboriginal theme, for one thing. Carved soapstone, a little wooden totem pole, two large carved masks on the walls. Semi-hidden along a wall in the rear of the house, in the laundry room—how did they do that in a floating house?—was a wall of framed artworks that looked like they'd been done by amateurs. She would have guessed his children, except he'd never mentioned having any.

The sound of water being shut off startled her from her reverie and she hurried out of the back to find Macaulay coming downstairs in jeans and a bathrobe, rubbing his hair. His skin glowed ruddy under the tan. His deep-set eyes looked less troubled than usual. Even his face, which she'd come to think of as less chiseled than gaunt, had relaxed to a kind of easy softness that spoke of a happier him that she longed to explore.

"Your turn," he said as he padded to the kitchen. "I laid out some extra clothes in the bathroom. And I'm going to make some lunch, so don't take too long."

Bursting with questions that would have to wait, Kylie headed for the stairs.

# 16

B Y THE TIME HE HEARD KYLIE finish her shower and come downstairs, Mac's good mood had vanished.

It wasn't the memories of her last time here or the constant irritation of his ripped leg and the tenderness in his hip. And god knew it wasn't the way Kylie looked in the old jeans of Alyssa's he'd found lying in the back of his closet—the ones with the embroidered pink butterflies plunging suggestively down the front and rear. Kylie wore those, a pair of his wool socks, and his blue flannel shirt, the sleeves rolled up about eight times. She'd washed her long hair and pulled it back, still damp, so that her face, devoid now of any makeup, made him think of someone fresh off a farm. Only not any farm he'd ever been on. This was one of those fabled farms from the American Midwest that grew up beautiful spunky girls who headed out to take over the big city. Innocent but not.

He remembered how not.

"What is it?" she said when she saw his face.

"A phone call," he said.

"From?" She swayed over in her sock feet as if to see what he was cooking on the stove. But he could see from the way the blue flannel shirt moved on her that she wasn't wearing a bra. And the shirt wasn't buttoned to the top.

Mac pulled his robe tighter around him and moved quickly away from the tomato soup he'd been stirring. He went to the cupboard for some bowls. When he turned back, she was leaning back against the counter by the stove, her arms folded under her breasts, stretching the shirt down taut over them.

"The call was from Leonid," Mac said. "He said the police had been around to question him about the guy trying to run you down in his lot. They also casually asked if he knew anything about the MP who was killed on the Sea-to-Sky highway yesterday."

"MP?"

"Minister of Parliament. Kind of like one of your state senators. He was apparently on his way up to Milaya Ridge to hold a televised scrum about Tibor's plans to expand to the north side of Schlatter. Seems there's a natural bear habitat over there."

"And the man dies before he gets there," Kylie said. "Convenient for Tibor."

"The police thought so. But that's not all." Mac hesitated a moment, wondering whether to tell her something Leonid had probably meant to be kept in confidence. But hell, with what Leonid had just asked of him this afternoon, the old Russian had lost all his rights to that sort of tight control.

"Some of Leonid's workers were attacked this afternoon at about the same time someone tried to run you down. The attackers stole a barge—a wide-body, flat decked thing used for hauling shipping containers from shore to ship sometimes."

Kylie looked at him and he could see she was nonplused. "Did he report it?"

Mac shook his head. "Mistrust of authority runs deep in a lot of Russian immigrants. Can't imagine why. But also, one of his workers thought he recognized two of the thieves. He thinks they were Tibor's men."

Mac let that hang, saw her frown and start to work through the implications while he toasted four pieces of bread and spread on a tuna-and-cheese mixture he'd thrown together, then popped the open-faced sandwiches in the oven.

By the time he'd taken them out and served them, bubbling, on the table with the tomato soup, he saw she'd run through probably as many possibilities as he himself had.

"You think it's connected to the development of Milaya Ridge," she said as she sat down.

He picked up his spoon and gestured for her to start eating. "I'm beginning to think everything is."

"Even my sister's kidnaping?"

Her hand suddenly flew to her mouth as if she'd remembered something. She stood up from the table and hurried to the front door where she'd left her shoes and purse. She came back with a piece of folded Milaya Ridge stationery and handed it to him.

He opened it and read Samantha Michaelson's scrawled plea for help. It made his fears sink like a lump into the pit of his stomach. Though he hadn't confessed it to Kylie, there had been a part of him that had hoped Kylie's sister and the other young women had gone to Milaya Ridge of their own free will and were being paid well for their services. But add this to the memories of their drugged-like behavior, the guards Tibor had stationed around his inner door at the party, the way he'd kept Kylie away, and it all led to a grittier truth.

"Tibor's six Japanese guests," he said, and handed the note

back. "I've been thinking they might be the key to some of this. Do they know these women are being held against their will? Some of them anyway. Do they care? Who are they?"

He began eating his soup. Then he felt Kylie's eyes on him and looked to see her face filled with desperate hope. He cringed and ate faster. That look was too similar to how his clients used to look at him. Like Mac could solve all their problems.

He used to believe he could.

Kylie seemed to get it and look away. When he next checked her out, she'd sat back in her chair and was thoughtfully chewing her way through one of the cheese melts.

"We have two of their names," she said suddenly.

"What?"

"Of the Japanese. We have two of their names. Actually three. I caught a third in a conversation they were having at that party in Tibor's upper room last night. Yamamoto Hosyu. The guy who guided me down was Maruyama Jun. The guy you helped was Sato Hachiuma. "

Mac stared at her. "How do you do that?"

She raised her eyebrows at him.

"You speak Japanese?" he pressed.

She smiled and licked her lips. "Samantha was the language girl. I just remember names. It's a job skill. I meet a lot of people."

"Uh-hunh." Small-town girl. Big-time brains. "And we should do what with these names?"

"Your computer upstairs—it's hooked up to the internet?"

He nodded.

"Then let's finish our lunch and I'll show you."

Ten minutes later they were upstairs, with Kylie seated at the computer, blithely pretending no interest in the framed pictures or stacks of papers she'd been given only a glimpse of the day before. While Mac, in turn, pretended no interest at all in the way his flannel shirt gaped invitingly when she leaned over the keyboard. Or the way she smelled of his shampoo, but with a whole difference undertone when it wafted from her. Or the warmth of her body in this chilly upstairs office. The lightness of her fingers on the keys and computer mouse. The quickness of her eyes and mouth as she brought up his web browser and typed in a search engine address he didn't recognize.

"You don't do people searches?" she asked as she waited for it to come up.

He shook his head. "Used to use Quicklaw. Google. Now mostly just e-mail, newspapers, entertainment listings."

The search page was up and she entered the names one at a time, using Boolean operator symbols he recognized from Quicklaw to list alternative spellings and word orders.

Nothing on the first. A bewildering blizzard on the Jun name, that seemed to go all over the map, many of the pages coming up in Japanese, untranslatable.

"Do you want me to—?"

"Try just the last name 'Sato' narrowed by business, foreign investment, ski hill, Milaya Ridge ," Mac said on a hunch. Sato-san, as his escort had called him, had been easily the oldest of the Japanese there, and the only one others had seemed to defer to.

Kylie shrugged and typed in the name, with narrowing words. Just five web sites came up. Kylie clicked on them in a way that made each open in a new window on the screen. She quickly eliminated three that talked about some Japanese sports hero who seemed to be in his teens and liked to ski. Kylie made the last two come up full-screen one at a time.

The first described Hachiuma Sato as a successful businessman who'd just helped finance a new school in a suburb of Tokyo. The second was an expose on the Yakuza. Sato's name was mentioned as a probable Oyabun, or head of a Yakuza clan.

"Yakuza?" Mac said. "The Japanese mafia? Now what would Tibor want with them?"

"A coalition?" Kylie suggested. "Because he's Russian mafia?"

Mac shook his head. "Tibor's solo mean, not mafia."

"But Leonid..."

"Is clean," Mac said. He'd better be.

Kylie stared at him a moment. "Then why go Yakuza? Why not look for legitimate investors?"

Mac pondered that and his discussion with Leonid earlier in the day. "Because he's gone through all the legitimate investors and they've turned him down."

"They figure Milaya Ridge is a money pit."

Mac raised his eyebrows at her.

~~~~

Okay, Kylie thought. Here goes.

"Leonid's secretary told me," she said carefully. "She said Leonid's lawyer sold him on it against Leonid's explicit advice and is still working on it with him."

Macaulay's face blanched white and he straightened up behind her chair.

She had to know. "Was that you, Mac? *Is* that you?"

He looked at her with his face set in a grim white line. "No."

Kylie bit her lip. "I saw you yesterday, you know. Following that black limousine that cruised past the accident on the Sea-to-

Sky highway. Were the Japanese in that limo?"

Macaulay nodded tensely. "Did you happen to see who was driving the car I rode in?"

"No, but..." A memory flashed of a woman sitting in the back. Alyssa! Which meant... "Your brother?"

Mac nodded again. "I told you he was a lawyer too. Corporate. He seems to think that Milaya Ridge is his ticket to the big time."

"So you're not Leonid's lawyer in this?"

Mac frowned and shook his head. "I told you I don't do law any more. And I was in litigation, suing for people who were hurt. What would I be doing with something like Milaya Ridge?"

"You tell me. What *are* you doing for Leonid Balakirev."

Macaulay's mouth closed tightly and he shook his head.

"You can't tell me."

"Or won't," he said ironically, mimicking the accusation she'd flung at him the last time she was here. He took a step back and crossed his arms over his chest like he was waiting for her to stomp out again.

For a few seconds Kylie considered it. How could she trust or work with a man who was keeping things from her? Then she studied his face and saw the pain there. She remembered he'd already helped her find Samantha. He'd saved her life and risked his own to catch the man trying to kill her. And he'd loved her last night up in the Creekside in a way too open to be an act.

How could she *not* trust him? And what other choice did she have when every part of her ached to be with him? She'd seen him respond to her ever since her shower. He might think he was hiding it well, but every so often, when he wasn't thinking hard through this puzzle, his gaze wandered over her body and tingled everywhere it touched.

She could feel her nipples growing taut under his borrowed shirt even now as she thought about it.

"Turn on your printer," she said at last.

"Pardon?"

"I want to print this out and some pages on the Yakuza. See if there are things we should know, things to look for that would confirm these guys actually are."

He walked to the printer, flicked it on, she began printing, and he said, "You know who we need to speak to next, to confirm this?"

Kylie looked up, puzzled by the pain in his voice. "Who?"

He dropped his eyes to the floor. "My brother."

# 17

Downstairs, Kylie popped a mint in her mouth, slid open the sliding glass doors, and walked out onto his back "patio" while Macaulay made the phone call in the living room.

She closed the glass doors behind her and walked to an unguarded edge of the five foot wide patio stip. She looked down at the water lapping the house's foundations. My goodness. It was still chilly, but only Vancouver chilly. The sun burned in a brilliant clarity above. The temperature was above freezing.

Kylie wrapped her arms around her and sucked on her mint with a kind of excited expectation. This place, the ski resort in Milaya Ridge, they were all a weird fantasy. Danger seemed just under the surface of everything. Nothing was certain. And Kylie had not felt this alive since the first time she'd left Madison at twenty-one.

She heard the patio door open and turned to see Macaulay come out in his bare feet.

"He's finally back in his office, but he can't see us until six," he said. "That gives us about four hours. You want to swing by your hotel, pick up some of your clothes? I can show you the town."

"We could do that," Kylie said, but made no attempt to move.

"Or...we could just stay here and watch the boats."

She looked out at False Creek and noticed the regular traffic on it for the first time. Sailboats and little putt-putts. People waved from one of the latter as they passed. "Neighbors?" she asked.

He nodded with a funny look on his face. Then she realized what it must look like—her wearing his oversized shirt and these obscene jeans; him in his bathrobe.

And she suddenly felt the anticipation in him, identified the excitement in herself. She gave him a slow, wide smile and he looked nervously away from her. She almost laughed. It was such a reversal from the night before. Had that only been last night?

Her skin tingled. Last night had been magical, but rushed. Too male. And just now Macaulay had said they had almost five hours before they had to leave.

"I'm chilly," she said, finishing her mint. "Let's go inside."

~~~~

Mac nodded, dry-mouthed, and let her lead.

Inside, as soon as he'd shut the patio door, she gently took his hand and pulled him towards the stairs.

"Can I see your bedroom again?" she asked.

He tried to laugh but it came out like a hiccup. "Do I have a choice?"

"There's always a choice." Her eyes held his as she said it, probing deeply until she smiled and tugged his hand again.

As she walked up the stairs ahead of him, he was hit with an uncomfortable flashback of Alyssa, wearing those same pants, that same top, leading him up with almost the same aggressive demand. My god, they *were* similar. They were both compact sexual beasts, smart, driven. And they both knew how to pull him by his head, heart, and little second head just above his legs.

Correction, Alyssa *had* known how to pull him. *Had*, past tense. And proven that, for all that, she didn't know him at all. She'd bailed at his first sign of weakness.

So what was he doing exposing himself like this again, to the same sort of woman?

They were at the door of the bedroom, Kylie still holding his hand. She turned and looked at him, licked her lips, then kicked open the door and led him inside.

He tugged himself to a stop short of the bed. Unable to stop himself, he looked to his chest of drawers and the framed eight-by-ten of Alyssa sitting on top of it.

Kylie saw the look, sucked in her lips for a moment, then let go of his hand and walked to the picture. Ever so gently, she lifted it and laid it face down on the dresser top.

"I'm not her," she said. "And she's not here. It's just you and me, Mac. If you want me."

~~~~

She looked at him, quivering inside so hard she felt like she'd burst, but unwilling to back down. Strange she hadn't even considered Mac's ex-wife in all this.

How long had they been divorced? Three years? That was nothing. And by his account, it was Alyssa who had left him. From this house. Probably from this bed that Macaulay and Alyssa had shared as man and wife.

Was Mac ready to take Kylie there now?

Because if he wasn't, if he turned her down right now when she'd finally been willing to put away her own mistrust, would she ever be able to open herself to him again? To anyone ever again?

~~~~

*Take her!* his dependable little second head screamed as his mind and heart debated fiercely with each other.

On the one hand, he'd felt a tangible flood of relief when Kylie had understood and done exactly the right thing. Going to the dresser, turning over Alyssa's picture, robbing the witch of her power.

On the other hand, it didn't change the fact of what Kylie was asking him to do. She wanted him to make love to her in this house, in this bed. He'd had one night stands since Alyssa left, but none of those women had gripped his being like Kylie did. None of them had so threatened his sense of balance.

"If I...," he started weakly.

She began walking to him, unbuttoning the flannel shirt she wore as she came. He blinked his eyes closed for a moment. When he opened them, she was directly in front of him, the shirt sliding from her arms. Her eyes regarded him calmly. His own gaze roamed down over her skin. Still taut from the cold downstairs, he could see little goose bumps down her arms. Her breasts rose and fell like ripe grapefruits before him, the nipples puckered up hard.

"I...," he tried again. "I-yai-yai."

She grabbed the front of his robe firmly in her hands and pushed him backwards until his calves bumped the bed. "Sit," she ordered.

He sat.

Then, still holding him by the front of his robe, she stood with her legs on either side of his and brought her face down to his own. Her breath was a sweet whisper in his nose. Her lips brushed his. *Warning! Warning! Fire!* exploded through him, urging he escape and paralyzing him at the same time, finishing in a cold rush right up his spine.

She brushed her lips over his again, wet this time, and he sucked in her heat, wondering when he'd shaved last. Her lips were so smooth. They demanded. His entire face tingled, alive.

On the third pass, she let her lips linger and slide, and he found his own reaching eagerly against them, his whole being concentrated there.

When she pulled back and looked into his eyes, for a moment he almost couldn't see her. He felt blind, a thing of sensation only.

She nodded and kissed him again, her tongue sliding briefly into his mouth and making his brain explode again, urging him to reach out for her.

But as he, she grabbed his arms and pressed them gently back. Lips still pressed to his, she reached down, found the sash of his robe and tugged it until it loosened. She drew back just enough to see as her hands spread the folds apart, fingers running lightly over his skin, pushing the sides back and down over his arms.

His own skin, he saw was as taut as hers. Darker, covered with a soft thatch of chest hair, but his nipples poked out like mini versions of her own. His skin felt the electricity of her body, her hands, what she was building between them.

"Lie back," she said, and he obeyed without question. His arms were free of the robe and it lay in soft crumples beneath him.

He gasped a little as he felt her fingers on the clasp of his jeans, tugging, separating the top, pulling the zipper down, sliding her fingers around the top of his underwear. Then, as he watched the exciting sway of her breasts, she stepped back and pulled hard to slide both jeans and jockey shorts down his legs and off.

Before he could wonder at his nudity before her, she was back to him and pushing his rising torso back onto the bed. In little, maddening nips and kisses, she took her mouth around his ears and down his neck.

He groaned as she reached his chest and smoothed her hands again over his shoulder, her pulled back hair spilling sideways to brush his nipple. She gently but firmly pushed down his reaching arms.

Working her lips in hot breaths and kisses over his chest, she stopped where her hair had tickled before—his right nipple. With a sudden stab and swirl of her tongue, she possessed it completely, ending in a quick nip that made him half-convulse and try to grab her again.

But again she pushed his arms back. And this time, after attacking his second nipple, she ran her fingers lightly down his ribs, slowing the pace of her kisses and nips to almost nothing... when one of her hands suddenly swooped in over his groin to grab his erection tightly.

He felt himself jerk in her hands, his buttocks tightening, his breath coming faster.

He made himself relax and focus again on her mouth. It was down to his belly now, kissing, tonguing gently, bringing his awareness to parts of himself rarely noticed.

Then the lips stopped, though the warmth was still there, the feel of her making him feel parts of himself he'd never noticed before. And she took him into her mouth in one great rush of heat.

"Oh...my...god," he groaned.

~~~~

For a moment Kylie felt a rush of fear. Mac wasn't a towering man, but he suddenly seemed huge, all of him—the muscles of his chest, his arms, his stomach, chiseled hard. And now this, this gloriously male appendage that bucked and quivered in her hands and mouth, that seemed pumped with blood like the rest of him.

Then her exhilaration returned. Yes, Macaulay Rush was powerful. Like a jungle cat, a calculating, supremely confident wild beast. And she controlled him. With her body, with her scent and touch and words and taste—she had made him hers.

She used her tongue and hands now, stoking his furnace, feeling his body temperature rise, his muscles squirm for release. But she wasn't going to let that happen easily. Not this time.

Sensing his mounting loss of control, she pulled back and rose off him. His gaze was riveted to her, watching her with feral hunger. And again she sensed what she'd felt last night in Milaya Ridge. Macaulay might be unwilling to share all his secrets about his work, his relationship with the Balakirevs, but in this sphere at least, he had nothing to hide.

Sliding back off the bed, Kylie undid her borrowed jeans and slid them casually down and off. She hadn't worn any underwear, knowing, even before she'd admitted it to herself, where this day had been headed.

With only Mac's socks on, she faced him more unabashed than she'd ever faced a man. Because she was in control here. He waited on *her*. She thrust one hip out, put a fist on the other, and asked the question that designers and managers of clothing lines were always asking of her: "Do you like what you see?"

Oh, so casual. Inside she quivered near fainting.

"Beyond words," Mac croaked.

"Good answer," she said in a rush. "Very good."

She strutted to the bed and climbed on, shuffling forward on her knees until they were on either side of his chest. "Now I think it's time you proved it."

Because of Mac's prodigious intellect, he obviously got the hint. His hands suddenly grabbed her bum from behind and his head came up to her sweet spot. She felt his grizzle on her inner thigh, rough and exiting. Then heat from his breath, fingers reaching in from behind to touch her wetness. And his tongue suddenly connected to her sex like a live plug.

Kylie bucked much as Mac himself had earlier, but he didn't stop *her* hands as she grabbed the back of his head, pulling him into her, shaking and writhing under his attentions, finding the rhythm of him, riding the incredible sensations.

She felt herself impossibly cresting in what seemed only minutes. And then again twice more, in little cascades she almost didn't recognize.

It rushed adrenaline through her muscles, making them clench and release until she was too exhausted to stay upright. She threw herself sideways onto the bed, taking him by surprise.

He looked at her wide-eyed. Wide green eyes, she saw, flecked with brown and gold in the sunlight from the window. "Are you alright?" he said.

She nodded with a laugh. "Your turn," she said, and spread her legs apart.

# 18

AFTER HE WAS DONE, a surprisingly gentle, rhythmic act that near the end became furious and almost sent Kylie over the top again, they lay with her on top of him.

They'd flung the covers off the bed at last and lay on the sheets.

Kylie turned her head to rest sideways on Mac's chest and looked out the window, whose blinds, she only now seemed to notice, were wide open. She could see the sailboats and skiffs passing. She could look across at the sun-glinted windows of the condos ringing the downtown core.

"People could have watched this whole thing," she murmured.

"I figured you wanted that."

She jerked her head up to look at him. "What?"

He grinned. "Showing off. Staking your claim. Something like that."

"Why you...conceited..." She swiped at him but he grabbed her hands and rolled her off him, then was on top of her, stretching her arms up over her head, nuzzling her, making her own legs squirm, and threatening to start the whole orgy they'd just been through all over again.

"No. No. Wait," she managed.

He backed off with another grin. "What?"

"This is talking time."

"About your sister?"

She shook her head. "Soon. First I want to know more about you." He pulled back warily but she wrapped her arms around the small of his back. "You told me last night that you took on one desperate case too many and lost. Tell me about that case."

He looked down at her and all the hurt and hooded nature she'd first seen in his eyes flooded back into them. Oh, no, she thought. She'd done it again. She'd pushed too hard and he was going to walk on her again. Even now. Ever after going through this twice, getting their hearts even more tangled. Kylie unconsciously tightened the grip of her fingers over the small of his back.

"Let me go," he said at last.

Her heart ready to cry out, Kylie nonetheless released her fingers and he slid quickly off her. Without reaching for any of his clothes, he stalked out of the bedroom. She heard a creak of another door in the hall, a shuffle of moved papers that told her it was his office he'd entered, then the sound of his returning steps.

He stopped, naked, beside the bed, and tossed the framed photograph of the young girl down on it, the one who reminded Kylie of Samantha when Sam was a kid.

"Melanie Carson," Macaulay said. "When she was ten, her mother tried to commit suicide by driving her car over the edge of a bridge into a river. Melanie and her little brother, Gary, were in the car at the time. The mother and Gary died. Somehow the cold water kept Melanie alive long enough for rescue crews to pull her out alive."

Kylie put her fingers to her mouth, almost wishing he'd stop, but he went on, his voice hard and flat.

"Melanie's dad, who'd only been seeing the kids ever second weekend at this point, brought Melanie to me because I'd developed a reputation for helping clients with mild traumatic brain injuries.

"She might or might not have had one of those. What she did have was psychological damage—panic attacks, inability to concentrate, overwhelming fatigue that turned into chronic fatigue syndrome and fibromyalgia, ongoing generalized pain."

He seemed momentarily lost, remembering. "What did you do?" Kylie prompted.

"Got her help," Mac said, and began pacing around the room. "We sent her for counseling, medical assessments, private tutoring. We started a lawsuit against the mother's insurance."

"And?"

"Melanie got worse. The insurers refused to pay anything but a pitiful settlement for 'emotional suffering.' Turns out the father had a history of psychological problems and abusing his kids. Therefore Melanie must have had 'preexisting emotional damage.' Can't establish a causal link to the accident."

He was beating his fingers against his forehead now as if he could beat the memories into some other shape.

"What about, what did you call it? Chronic fatigue? Her chronic pain?"

He looked at her with his eyes haunted. "Ah, yes. Chronic fatigue and fibromyalgia. I'd had two other cases of that. It usually hits high-achieving, stressed-out women, not little girls. But you know what? Half the medical profession believes it's strictly psychosomatic at best, malingering at worst. Insurers don't buy it. Juries don't buy it. Luck of the draw whether a judge will. Guess where my luck was with Melanie."

He turned from her with his whole body tense. She could see it rippling through him. One of his mid-back muscles twitched in spasm. His hands formed and re-formed fists.

"Did you go to trial?" Kylie asked quietly.

He let out a little cry and shook his head. "The insurance company targeted me on this case. They threw everything at me. Their two top lawyers, a half-dozen legal assistants. They papered me to death, brought motions in one courtroom while I was arguing in another. Managed to get the trial date pushed back three times, dragged it out over four years, hoping I'd just run out of money. Because this is all contingency work for us, of course. We lose, we get nothing. Most of the rest of my practice was going down the toilet, while our costs for reports and helping Melanie, my time alone..." He jabbed a thumb shakily at the ceiling.

"But I was going to fight them anyway, damn it. Right to the wall. For Melanie's sake. I had experts and lay witnesses out the wazoo. I had a messed-up, sympathetic plaintiff. I had legal research to sink a battleship. Then, the night before trial, I got a call from Jerome Smythe, the counsel on the other side. Same firm now representing Milaya Ridge resorts, incidentally. The firm my brother's in now."

"Oh, no," Kylie breathed. "What?"

"We got Lananaskis."

"That's a person?"

"A judge. One who is so thoroughly anti-plaintiff you pretty much have to roll your client into court in a body cast before he'll believe they're hurt. Needless to say, he doesn't believe in chronic fatigue or fibromyalgia. Jerome can hardly keep from laughing on the phone. He repeats his offer to settle, but cuts it down now to a nuisance fee. Enough to buy Melanie a cup of coffee and release us without having to pay the defendant's costs, which would have taken every last cent Melanie had."

He turned and looked at her and Kylie shrank back at the ugliness in his face. "I took the offer."

"But," Kylie said and swallowed, "couldn't you fight, then appeal?"

"Appeals are for errors in law. A smart judge can make himself unappealable in a case like Melanie's. Lananaskis is cruel and cold, but he's smart. No. Smythe had outmaneuvered me, that's all. Called in favors. Unethical but unprovable. He played the game better."

Mac's voice had gone cold again, and his face totally completely blank it was like Kylie wasn't there. It sent chills down her spine. "Mac...," she pleaded. "Please don't shut me out."

He looked at her icily, then seemed to give a little shake and the pain returned to his eyes. "I'm sorry," he said. "It's not a place I like to go. Not easy admitting you don't measure up."

"Or that the *system* doesn't," she said. "Not you."

"Whatever." He walked to where his robe lay crumpled on the bed and scooped up it and his jeans and underwear. "I'm getting dressed. I need a walk before I go to see John. It'll keep me from spitting in his face."

~~~~

Macaulay threw on his jeans, runners, and a heavy green sweatshirt to take his walk alone, while Kylie anxiously paced his house. When an hour passed and he still hadn't come back, she considered getting in her car and driving back to her hotel.

But something kept her in Mac's house. She wasn't going to run this time. He could, but she wouldn't.

Instead, she set about cleaning his kitchen. Then she freshened up, did her hair, and washed out her blouse and underwear from earlier that day. She could hardly go on info-gathering to a lawyer's office in no makeup and Mac's flannel shirt. She decided she *would* wear Alyssa's old jeans instead of her too tight skirt, on the other hand. The jeans made a statement. Because they were jeans. Because they were suggestive. Because they were Alyssa's. Because she'd seduced Mac in them.

Mac.

She examined her feelings about what he'd told her and admitted that even though she was still powerfully drawn to him, he had definitely pricked the over-swollen balloon of her regard for him. He was a wounded man. Despite all his obvious intelligence and strength, Macaulay Rush was as damaged, in his way, by what had happened to Melanie Carson as the little girl had been herself.

It had destroyed his nerve. It had cost him his career, his wife, probably most of his friends too, since she noted he never talked about having any.

And had it been like he said? Was he just not a good enough lawyer? Not tough enough for the game? Was that why he'd let himself be sucked under the control of Leonid Balakirev? Why wouldn't Mac tell her what he was doing for the man?

When he still hadn't returned by a quarter to five, Alyssa went up to his office and turned his computer back on. Fully aware of the trust she was breaking, she began going through his computer files, bringing up document after document she shouldn't have been able to get. Melanie Carson's entire case, for example, all their pleadings, the affidavits he'd drafted...

It was as if Macaulay had no conception of computer security, or simply didn't care. Even if all these client files were settled or closed, they should still have been locked away or deleted. She'd have to talk to him about that.

Then a directory marked "TB" caught her eye. But when she clicked on it, she was asked to enter a password.

So he did have security. For important things like TB. Tibor Balakirev?

A banging sound downstairs startled her and she quickly shut down the computer and left the room. She descended the stairs to find Macaulay bustling around in the kitchen, putting away a bag of groceries. His face was flushed from the cold. His hair was windblown.

"Long walk," she said from the bottom stair.

He jerked up and turned around. "I figured you'd be gone by now."

"Nope. You said we were going to question your brother at six. That's in half an hour."

He turned from Kylie's steady gaze. "I can do that alone."

"She's my sister."

He paused, about to say something, then nodded. "All right. We'll take your car."

Something suddenly struck her. "Don't you have a car?"

"I do. I just don't have it insured. I'd offer to drive us there on my motorcycle, but it's been in a little accident. Are you going like that?"

She smiled sweetly back at him. "I am. Are you going like that?"

~~~~

By the time they'd parked under the Scotia Tower where John worked and gone up to the sidewalk to enter from the street level, Mac found he'd almost reconciled himself to Kylie being with him.

He'd been frankly astonished to find her still in his house when he'd come back. Ever since losing Melanie's case and going into an emotional tailspin, it had become par for the course for people to drop away from him. It was some kind of animal instinct—abandon the sick and feeble.

But Kylie Michaelson was obviously not your typical animal. Despite her sexy, somewhat egocentric nature, despite having some issues about her parents and sister, she'd come all the way up to Canada to hunt for Samantha, kind of a needle-in-a-haystack search he'd thought until recently.

Then she'd asked that, no *insisted* that, he tell her what drove him. But only after she'd aggravated, prodded, snuck around, and then seduced him right in his own home, wearing his ex-wife's jeans, in his ex-wife's bed.

And she hadn't left afterwards.

She hadn't left.

It almost made him want to take that final step and tell her everything.

"Rapney, Smythe, Walker. Is that it?" Kylie asked. She was scanning the list of the buildings tenants. Even in jeans, he noted, the high heels she wore made her legs look exceptionally taut and long. But she filled out the worn denim better than Alyssa's stick legs ever had. She made those jeans hers. She was making his heart hers.

*Tell her.*

He nodded. "That's it."

"They have two floors."

"John's on the twentieth."

So that moment for telling passed for then as they walked through the crowd of exiting business suits to grab a free elevator and go up.

But still, he thought, if there was anyone he wanted beside him as he set up his plans for Tibor's downfall, Kylie was it.

# 19

Y OU'VE GOT A HELLUVA NERVE, Mac," said the young lawyer Kylie recognized as John Rush from the picture in Macaulay's office and the brief sighting in Tibor's upper room in Milaya Ridge.

"Answer the question," Mac said.

The two brothers squared off over the younger one's glass desk, ultra-modern but still piled with papers beside the computer set up and phone. Kylie and Mac had woven through what seemed like a mile of other offices and cubicles to get back here. The staff still working had buzzed in a hushed frenzy when they'd passed.

What? They'd never seen Mac Rush breeze in for a visit with a jeans-clad babe in his wake before? Or maybe they recognized the jeans.

Whatever the effect Kylie's appearance had worked in the general office offices of Rapney, Smythe, though, she was almost invisible in here. These two boys obviously had some issues that Mac's visit was bringing to the surface.

"You want me to lay out all the financials?" John said, his voice rising, his face red. "The investors are public knowledge;

everything's been filed. You want me to show you the bank loans and investor statements?"

"I just want you to tell me, straight out," said Mac, "when you expect this giant turkey to turn a profit."

"Milaya Ridge is not a turkey."

"Then when?"

"I'm not an accountant!"

"But you're an investor, aren't you. How much do you personally have tied up in this, John?"

John's mouth opened like he was about to blurt an answer, then he snapped it shut.

"Come on," Mac prodded. "You said it was going to make you rich. You weren't just talking about partnership, or taking over Jerome's office. This is your ticket up. This is the answer to Alyssa's wet dreams."

Kylie gasped at the crudeness and John said, "Shut up, Mac."

"How far's she got you into debt, bro'?"

"Shut up."

"Does she still like her Super Sundays where she sees how many stores she can clean out in four hours? Does that still get her hot? Does she come home and show her appreciation to you right there on the couch or kitchen floor?"

"Screw you."

"Milaya Ridge, John. It's stalled, isn't it? Even with Jackson Pollard dead, I bet all your investment deals are falling through. Something about targets not met? Approvals not received?"

"How did you—?"

"Because they all know, don't they, that the resort's not sustainable at its current size and Tibor just isn't going to get the permits to expand. That's why he's gone after Yakuza investors."

John, who'd looked like he was about to leap his desk and strangle Mac, suddenly blinked in confusion, shaking his head as if he hadn't heard right. "Pardon me?"

"The Yakuza," Mac repeated. "The six Japanese 'gentlemen' you helped escort past Jackson Pollard's burning corpse on the highway. What's Tibor expect them to do for him? Just money? Or are they going to bring a little more gang-style pressure on people holding up development?"

"Yakuza..." John brow was still scrunched, like he had a serious pain he was trying to put away. He looked directly at his brother and seemed about to speak when the door of his office swung open and a handsome white-haired man in his sixties stuck in his head.

"Trouble, John?" Without waiting for an answer, he flashed a quick, disingenuous smile at Macaulay. "Hello, Mac."

"Jerome," said Mac. Kylie could hear the loathing.

"No trouble, Jerome," said Mac.

"Good. Good," said the man Kylie remembered now from Mac's story about Melanie Carson. Jerome Smythe, one of the law firm's partners. He'd been the lawyer defending the insurance company. The one who'd pulled strings to get the unfair judge. "Remember that if there's one person you can't trust it's a plaintiff's lawyer."

"I don't practice anymore," Mac said stiffly.

"Yes," said Smythe with an oily smile. "I heard that. Second worst person to trust, I believe, is a family member. Speaking of which..."

He pushed the door wide and stepped back. Alyssa Rush, ex-wife of Mac, current of John, strode regally into the room, dressed in upscale chic.

For a moment Kylie wished she could shrink into a little ball and roll into hiding in the corner. But then she took in the cold way Alyssa dismissed Smythe, and smiled coldly at John and Mac. Kylie saw Mac visibly blanch and step back uncertainly. Kylie's own spine stiffened and she straightened in her chair.

How dare Alyssa? How dare she win Mac in his prime, apparently wrap him around her little finger, then dump him at the first sign of weakness? And how dare John, with all his schoolboy charm, scoop her up before her place in Mac's bed was even cool?

Alyssa had pointedly ignored Kylie when she'd come in, but now she turned to her as if in surprise. "Why, Mac," Alyssa purred. "I see you've brought along your snow bunny. Isn't she a little young for you?"

"Or John for you?" Kylie said, pointedly not getting up.

"Cute. The little thing is so cute. And I do recognize the pants. So very coy ten years ago when I bought them on Robson. Mac *was* always keen to get into them."

"I'm sure he wasn't the only one."

"Oh, oh, oh. Verbal *touché*. I suppose one must learn to stab when wearing polyester."

"Rayon-viscose, actually," said Kylie. She rose slowly and walked up to Alyssa. Though she was shorter, she felt more solid here as she looked the older woman up and down. "Unlike, let's see...Prada sunglasses in tinted plastic, Bill Blass sweater-vest in a cotton-poly blend, A Shin Choi acetate top, costume pearl necklace and earrings, local designer broach, pleather pants, Anne Klein calf boots in brushed suede. Gucci canvas-and-leather purse."

Kylie looked at John with exaggerated pity in her eyes.

"Mac's right, you know. All expensive, but no designer loyalty and nothing really carries between lines. It's no wonder she's a compulsive shopper. She keeps trying to make things fit."

She looked back at Alyssa with a glint of gotcha but it caught in her throat when she saw the look of pure hate on the woman's face. Then the look passed and Alyssa swept away from her, walking behind John's desk and draping a hand over his shoulder.

"John, dear," she said, "we're due back at Milaya Ridge tonight, remember? Tibor made me promise we wouldn't be late. His guests are only here today and tomorrow."

John, his face still drawn in worry lines as if he'd missed Kylie's whole exchange with his wife, looked at Macaulay. "Yakuza?"

Mac nodded. "And the women Tibor's using to entertain them? At least some are doing it against their will, drugs involved."

John scoffed. "Tibor's not—"

"One of them sent Kylie here a plea for help letter this morning. This afternoon, a pickup truck with a driver wearing a ski mask tried to run Kylie over."

"Mac almost caught him," Kylie said quickly, "but he escaped back across the Lion's Gate Bridge."

"Still...," said John, less sure of himself.

"When they questioned us," Mac lied, "the police seemed pretty convinced that Jackson Pollard's death wasn't accidental. Tibor's name came up more than once."

There was a long silence. Finally Alyssa took a little breath. "Well, you can take a plaintiff lawyer out of the courtroom, but you can't convince him the big guys aren't evil. Conspiracy theories abound. Meanwhile *we*"—she grabbed John by the sleeve again—"are going to be late if we don't leave now." She smiled tightly at Mac and Kylie. "It's been charming to see you both."

John shook her off, his face sober. "Okay, look, Mac. Maybe something's going on here."

"Maybe?" said Mac.

"Well, *something* is. Either way, you might want to consider not going back to your place tonight. Or at least set up—Kylie, was it?—somewhere else."

"How about at the police station?" Mac said. "I promised to take her back there tonight to tell the cops everything we suspected about Tibor and the Yakuza."

Kylie wondered at the lie, but saw it panicked John.

"Hold off just a day on that, okay?" the younger brother said. "I'll talk to Tibor. I'll get the goods and get back to you. We'll figure this out."

He fumbled through his pants pockets, pulled out a set of keys, worked a small one free of the ring and handed it to Mac. "This lets the elevator access the underground mall after hours. You should go out that way in case someone's watching the front door."

"Ooooh," said Alyssa, waving her long nails up by her face. "Conspiracy. But I'll take that key anyway." She plucked it from Mac's fingers. "Because I just remembered that *I* need to buy some lip balm before we head out tonight. Let's go darlings. John, I'll meet you at the car."

She swept out.

After the briefest pause, Mac nodded at John, grabbed Kylie's arm, and followed her.

They'd ridden all the way down in uncomfortable silence with Alyssa and stepped out into the small hallway in the elevator basement. One of the doors she saw obviously joined up with the underground malls. Kylie could smell car exhaust and figured the garages where they parked must also be close.

Mac touched her arm. "I'm leaving you here," he said. "You go through that door, stay left, and you'll see signs to the garage we parked in. Can you find your way back to my place?"

"Yes, but..."

"One block east of it is a little Thai restaurant. I'm probably being paranoid, but go there and wait for me. Order us both some dinner. I'll be about half an hour behind you. I just have to take care of something urgent."

"With him," Alyssa drawled from where she'd been watching, "it's always urgent."

As much to spite Alyssa as anything, Kylie nodded and smiled. "Just one thing," she said.

"What?" Mac said.

She grabbed the front of his sweatshirt and pulled him close, planting her lips hotly on his and slipping in her tongue until she felt him start to respond. Then she drew back an inch, her nose still close to his. "No more than half an hour this time, okay?"

She felt him nod against her. "I promise," he said.

Then he was gone.

From behind her, Alyssa said in almost a sigh, "He always was a good kisser. Give him that much."

Kylie couldn't bring herself to respond. She just walked out the doors Mac had pointed her towards.

~~~~

Tibor's hit the Talk button on his cell phone before the first ring had finished. "Well?" he said.

"She's moving. Alone." The caller gave the exact directions and hung up.

153

Tibor pressed the second speed dial button on his phone, heard it answered immediately, and gave his directions. Then he clicked off the phone, slipped it back in his pocket, and stepped out of the doorway of the Gastown restaurant where he'd taken his Yakuza guests and their 'escorts' to eat.

On the cobblestone curb, Maksim was helping to usher his Yakuza guests and the girls into two limousines.

About to climb into the forward limo, the hopelessly pretty Samantha Michaelson swept back her blond hair and smiled at Ogano Sato behind her. Ogano leaned forward and nibbled at her ear, looking happy as a rutting pig. No doubt he'd told her of "his" plan to steal her away from Tibor tomorrow night. Probably he hoped she'd give him a preview of her delicacies tonight to cement the agreement.

And if he is happy enough, thought Tibor, tossing back his own hair, Ogano will insist his father, Hatchiuma Sato, ally this Yakuza family to Tibor's growing organization.

Then even Tibor's father would tremble in fear of him. Milaya Ridge would become almost an afterthought.

Ogano's right hand grabbed Samantha's behind as she stepped off the curb and ducked her head to enter the limo. She froze and drew back her head, her nostrils flaring.

Tibor hurried forward and put a hand on both Samantha's and Ogano's shoulders. "Please, you two," he said. "If you get too cozy, I might have to separate you. That would be a shame with such little time left to spend together, *nyet*?"

Samantha's head nodded quickly and she ducked in. Ogano smiled and winked at Tibor before he followed her.

Tibor narrowed his eyes. This Michaelson girl... It was good that he soon would have extra leverage to ensure her compliance.

*Disposable* leverage. Tibor had changed his mind about keeping Kylie; he'd had enough Michaelson women for one lifetime.

The cell phone hung heavy in his jacket pocket. He willed it to ring and tell him the task was done.

~~~~

Monday at 6:50 p.m. was not exactly a busy night in the mall. Everything at this end looked closed and shuttered. The occasional shop employee could still be seen tidying up inside the stores. A few workers from the office buildings around had obviously chosen to walk to their cars or dinner dates via the underground. But the whole place felt eerie.

Kylie walked faster, hearing the click-click of her high-heeled shoes against the tiles, the only clear sound other than the background hum of the overhead fluorescents and occasional scuffling conversations of people passing down another branch of the mall up ahead.

She could hear her own breath, foolishly high in her chest. Then came the tingle on the back of her neck, her paranoid body sure once again that she was being watched. Stalked.

Angry, she stopped herself dead in her tracks for a good scolding.

But as she did, she heard the distinct sound of a scuffle as someone nearby tried to stop as quickly.

Shooting her eyes right and left, she saw nothing. No one. Then, maybe fifteen yards ahead, just before a turn in the mall passage, she saw a garage parking sign that must have been where Mac had directed her. Her car was there. If she could just make that, there would be an attendant on duty, other people coming and going, her own rental car with locking doors.

Oh so casually, she reached down and slipped off her high-heeled shoes so she stood barefoot on the cold stone tiles. Then she sprinted forward.

She heard a grunt of surprise from behind, then running steps, heavy, pounding. She had a mind picture flash of Maksim, the big Russian who'd escorted her and Mac to the Creekside just last night. She remembered Mac insulting him, Maksim taking it. But Mac wasn't here now. It was just Kylie.

Kylie's running feet sped over something gritty and sharp as she approached the door for the garage. She hoped it wasn't broken glass. But she was running too hard, too terrified, to process.

The door. The feet getting closer behind her. Kylie's arms pumping hard, her hands clutching her shoes. Her purse flapped out and bumped against her charging hips. High school track and field. Early morning running she'd taken up when her regular gym had shut down for a month.

*Run!*

Then she was there. Her hands clutched the knob, wrenched it with a crazy fear it would be locked, felt it turn, and burst through.

Stairs going up.

Gulping air, she grabbed the handrail and sprinted up. There was a door with a push-bar opener at the first landing. She slammed her open palms against it, crashing it open even as she heard the crash of the door behind her down the stairs.

Kylie plunged through it, into the garage itself, almost in front of a car roaring up the ramp to the ground level. She threw herself sideways...

And someone grabbed her from the front.

Kylie shrieked, only to cut it off as she saw who it was. Reassuringly strong and tall, his short blond hair brushed back like prairie wheat, Bo Rhinegold smiled down at her.

"Hey, now, pretty lady," he said, looking not at all surprised. "Imagine meeting you here."

"B-Bo? What are you doing downtown? Here. Now."

"I'm here to meet you, of course."

"Me? Why would you be here to..." She let it trail off as she heard heavy footsteps behind her and heard heavy wheezy sounds, like the breathing of rhinoceros. Or the human Russian equivalent.

"Well now, it seems Mr. Balakirev was put out by your lack of thanks for his hospitality last night. So he sent us to bring you round so you could thank him."

He nodded to the heavy breather behind him and Kylie turned to discover she'd been wrong. It wasn't Maksim, whom she thought she'd seen at least a trace of sympathetic humanity in. It was his colder, hairier brother, Slava.

Moving fast for a big man, he shielded his groin from her sudden kick then covered her mouth before she could scream.

# 20

MAC HUNG UP THE PAY PHONE ON GRANVILLE, just down from the Scotia Tower, and swore softly. Leonid wasn't answering at any of his numbers.

The next logical step was to call the police, like he'd threatened John he'd do. He knew where Tibor and his abductees were now, after all. All back at the Lodge, no doubt up in Tibor's upper room like last night. Or, even if they were now in some other party room at the Milaya Ridge resort, or scattered among a few different condos, the police could easily block off the one resort road. What he was pretty sure they wouldn't do was get search warrants to search the whole resort. Not, at least, unless they had definite proof that someone was being held up there against their will...

Mac needed Samantha's note, the one Kylie had with her. In fact, he needed Kylie herself. A passel of cops were more likely to listen to a pretty female than a scruffy ex-lawyer.

He shrugged his sweatshirt around his shoulders feeling the chill of the evening air suddenly, and stepped away from the phone.

A second chill went through him, almost like a premonition, as he looked out to West Georgia and the traffic heading for Stanley Park, then the Lion's Gate Bridge, the north shore, and the highway up past Milaya Ridge. A battered old pickup truck rumbled past in the flow of traffic, a blond driver at the wheel. Kid. Vaguely familiar. Two heads in the front seat beside him. Woman and man?

Gone.

The feeling of ice was still there between his shoulder blades. The last time he remembered it this clearly was the night before the Melanie Carson trial. He'd been strung out on forty-six hours of no sleep, scrambling to get all his witnesses lined up, their accommodations and transportation arranged, his documents prepped, his examinations of Melanie designed to help her get through without breaking down. Then the phone had rung and he'd picked it up to hear Jerome Smythe sniggering on the other end of the line.

*Oops*, Smythe had said. *Seems we've had a change of trial judge. We're getting Lananaskis. You remember Lananaskis, I trust. Do you want to talk settlement now?*

Now he had that same feeling of ice down his back and he knew why. Kylie. He shouldn't have left her alone. Not for a minute.

Turning quickly, he jogged back towards the Scotia Tower and the parking garage where they'd parked coming out. If she'd been a little slow finding her car, maybe he could still catch her coming out and signal her over.

But the only Grand Am he saw before the garage was the wrong color and driven by some teenager bouncing his head to music Mac couldn't hear. Mac ducked into the parking garage and took the stairs up three levels to where they'd parked. He burst out the door, breathing hard. Stopped.

There was the Grand Am.

Where was Kylie?

Fighting an urge to panic, Mac slowly walked to the Grand Am and looked inside. There was no note, no sign that Kylie had returned here. In fact the rental agreement he'd pulled from her glove box on the way here to read—habit—was still on her seat where he'd tossed it when he'd gotten out.

Kylie had never made it back here.

Jogging quickly to the elevator, he punched the buttons to make sure they worked and she wasn't stuck somewhere between floors. Five seconds later, the door dinged open and he got in, punched ground level. When he reached it he went straight to the ticket operator's booth.

"Hey!" He rapped on the glass and the west-Asian looking man slid it open. "Did a brunette woman come by here looking for her keys or in some kind of distress? Leave some sort of message?"

The operator shook his head. "No."

"But cars have left here, right? In the last ten minutes or so?"

"Yes. Yes. All the time."

The ice between Mac's shoulder blades shot back full force as he saw in his mind's eye again a pickup truck rumbling through traffic. Blue. Three people crammed into the front. "Do you remember," he said slowly, "if one of them was a pickup truck? A blue pickup with three people in the front?"

The man frowned and looked down to the left, then up, then down, like he was following a fly. Finally he nodded. "Two men and a woman, yes. One of the men was *very* big." He held his hands out from his shoulders to demonstrate.

Mac's stomach clenched and he swore inside. "Do you have a surveillance camera that records their faces or license plates or anything?"

The man stuck his hand out of the booth and pointed up and right. Following the finger, Mac saw what could have been a camera box attached to the ceiling just back from the ticket booth.

"How do I get a look at that tape?"

The ticket booth operator looked confused.

"To see it. Check it out. Money?" He pulled out his wallet

The man's eyes darted back and forth, then he shook his head vigorously. "I give you a card. You call this number, okay?" So saying, he stuck a business card he'd pulled from somewhere out the window and waved it for Mac to grab. When he did, the man motioned for him to get out of the way. A lineup of cars wanting to exit had formed behind him.

So Mac backed off, thinking hard. Three choices now: go to the police, track down Leonid for help, go after Kylie himself.

Actually, Mac thought wryly as he hailed a cab, there was a fourth choice—all of the above.

He'd never been a man for half measures.

~~~~

On the Sea-to-Sky highway, winding up past the ferries of Horseshoe Bay, the twistiness of the coast road looked ominous and nauseating in the darkness of night.

Kylie felt her stomach grumble and was glad she hadn't eaten dinner after all. No, a nice romantic Thai dinner seated across from Macaulay Rush as he told her his plans to rescue Samantha, could hardly compare to this.

Her hands were cuffed together behind her back, the metal biting into her wrists. A rope went from the cuffs, through split between the truck's old bench seat and backrest, then under, to tie onto the rope that bound Kylie's bare feet together.

"Not that we think you'll try to escape or anything stupid like that," Bo had said while Slava bound her. "Cause we got your baby sister, don't we?"

"We?" Kylie grunted at the time, trying to make her wrists bigger like she'd read somewhere you could do if you needed to slide out of handcuff later. It had only made them shoot with pain when Slava closed the bracelets hard.

"The big T, of course. Mr. Balakirev. My sponsor."

"He sponsors your skiing," Kylie said, disbelieving.

"Costs money to train," Bo said. "Money for equipment, money for coaches, money to scare up sponsorships, enter competitions. It's not like snowboarding, you know, where they got Extreme Sports dropping their drawers to get in line with the cash."

"And for that..."

"I do anything the big T tells me to. I watched you, followed you, kept my employers up to date by cellphone. At first it was just to keep you away from finding your sister. Even the wining and dining and taking you skiing—now that was the fun part."

Now Kylie flashed back to that, analyzing where and how Bo had stalked her and diverted her. She needed, she realized, to prove to herself that Mac hadn't been involved in that. Despite the fact he'd been her biggest distraction. Despite his secret call in the middle of last night.

But as the oncoming headlights whipped past them and Bo found the turnoff for the even darker and windier stretch up into the mountains to reach Milaya Ridge, Kylie felt her hopes turning into darkness too.

Because every time something had turned her away from her sister, or attacked her directly, Mac had been there. Even Slava and Bo's abduction of her now. Who'd known she was coming down the elevator to the mall level? Who'd been right there with her and said goodbye and *just the right moment*? Yes, it could have been John Rush, Alyssa, or even that awful Jerome Smythe if he'd hung around John's door listening. But for them it would be a one-time shot. For Mac, the man who always seemed to have something dark to hide, it was a pattern.

*Oh, Mac,* she moaned inside. *Why?*

Twenty minutes later, the twinkling lights of the resort appeared around the bend and Bo drove his truck to the very front of the crowded parking lot to take one of the reserved-for-staff spaces. Slava bent forward and cut the rope around her ankles, more roughly than he needed to and careful to pin her feet to the floor with a giant hand as he did it. Then he slipped some of the same rubber-soled slippers onto her feet that Maksim had used the night before and dragged her out of the truck.

And no one noticed? Couldn't anyone *see* how she was being goose-stepped in with her hands behind her back?

"No noise now, beautiful," Bo whispered in her ear. "Any extra attention you draw now, your sister draws later."

This time they entered the Lodge by a rear door that took them through a kitchen storage area then up a back flight of stairs. On the second flight of stairs, they had to buzz their way in through a metal security door and emerged in a narrow hallway.

The muted crash of tambourines, shouts, laughter, and smells told her the Russian party from last night was underway again as if it had never stopped.

Slava shoved her down the hall then jerked her to a stop before a plain-looking door. To her surprise, she felt Slava playing with her cuffs behind her back and her abused wrists were suddenly free. Then the door opened in front of her to a dark room, and Slava pushed her forward.

"Be happy, darlin'!" Bo called as she stumbled and fell. "You finally found what you been searching for!"

Blinking blindly in the darkness, Kylie became aware she was not alone. There was someone else in here. Someone sniffing and crying softly. Kylie felt her way across the hard floor and felt a bare leg, scratched, female. As she ran her hand over it, its owner scrabbled backwards with a pathetic whimper. "D-don't," the girl said.

Kylie's heart sank into her gut. "Samantha?"

# 21

**W**HAT DO YOU MEAN, 'We'll see'?" Mac exploded.

Constable Marlin, of the Vancouver Police Department, stepped out of the parking garage's ticket booth where they'd just fast-forwarded through the critical half hour of security tape and seen the blue pickup truck drive out with three people in the front—Slava, the blond driver Mac recognized now as Bo Rhinegold, and the woman squeezed uncomfortably between them who just an hour earlier had given him a kiss he could still feel on his lips. Kylie. Kidnaped.

"I mean," said Marlin, "that the woman did not appear to be in any distress."

"So they threatened her. You couldn't see her hands. They looked tied behind her back."

"But you said she knew the two men."

"Yes, she did. I bet you know some bad men too, Officer. Does that mean if they kidnap you, you're automatically a voluntary passenger? She left her rental car behind, damn it! You think that's normal?"

The mustached officer held up a hand. "No need for bad

language, sir. I said we'd check it out. I came over here with you. We're checking it out."

Mac stepped back with him out of the way of a car exiting the parking garage. He coughed on the exhaust and felt his head whirring with the cold of the night. He hadn't eaten since that bite of soup at noon, he realized and his hunger was probably fueling some of what he felt now, but he didn't care.

"Take the tape," he snapped.

"Pardon, sir?"

"Sign a form and take the goddamn security tape back to your HQ. Review it with your superior. I want to be there when you tell him you have a report of an abduction, an abandoned vehicle, and a tape showing the abductee in the front of a pickup leaving a parking garage sandwiched between two men. Maybe to be raped. Maybe murdered. That'll look really good in the file when it all comes out in the paper later."

The policeman's right eye twitched. "You don't have the spelling of the woman's last name. You met her yesterday. You don't know where she's staying in town. She told you a tale about looking for her sister, convinced you the sister was being drugged and held by what? The Russian mob? To be a sex-slave for a Yakuza mobster?"

"That's right."

"But you never even saw this sister. You have no proof it's not all the product of a skilled con."

"I saw a photograph. And a note..."

"Not difficult for her to fake."

"To what end?"

"To get into your house? Did she ever get you to leave her alone in there? Did you search to find whether anything was taken?"

*My heart*, Mac wanted to say. And he knew how crazy it all sounded when laid out bluntly, but he knew something this police officer didn't. He knew Tibor Balakirev. He'd had dinner with him off and on over the last decade and watched him change from a snot-nosed, overprivileged son of a Russian immigrant success story, into a snot-nosed manipulator with big dreams and a willingness to use very old country tactics to make them happen.

It's what Leonid had 'hired' him to check out for him after Mac had done his crash and burn from the legal profession. Whether to save Mac or to save his son, or both, Leonid had pushed Mac to go undercover at Milaya Ridge and find out what was really going on there behind the scenes.

When Kylie had shown up with suspicions of her sister being kidnaped and taken there, when she'd identified the Japanese visitors as Yakuza, it was only one of the last pieces of the puzzle Mac had been putting together on his own.

But the last piece still wasn't clear for Mac, which is why he'd held back from telling Kylie everything. Because despite all the evidence of Tibor as the bad guy, the complexity behind this scheme with the Yakuza, the fact they'd been contacted at all, indicated a sophistication of thought that was simply beyond Tibor.

Mac *knew* Tibor. Tibor's approach was to hire thugs like Slava and Maksim to beat up people who got in his way. Even the idea of Milaya Ridge... Would Tibor ever have considered it if John hadn't pushed it on him?

And was John the one still driving everything now?

The agony of that, the shame of it, the hope it wasn't true, had kept Mac's mouth zipped with Kylie and was keeping him from spilling everything now.

"Look, Officer Marlin," he said, "all I can tell you is you are so dead wrong in this you won't know it until your entire career gets run up a flagpole like dirty underwear. There is something very dirty going on out at Milaya Ridge, involving at least two kidnappings, quite possibly the murder of MP Jackson Pollard, and maybe an alliance being set up to get a bunch of Yakuza working with the Russian mob. You blow it off and I'll make sure you're flying traffic meters for the next twenty years."

The older police officer looked him coldly in the eye, then took out his little brown flipbook. "Why don't you give me your contact information, sir, and I'll let you know what we come up with."

~~~~

Samantha sniffed loudly rubbed her nose back and forth on Kylie's arm. "No," she said in a husky little voice Kylie hardly recognized as her sister's. "No, Ogano's going to take me away from here tomorrow. He promised. It's just...just...Tibor caught us joking about him and pulled me away, had Slava slap me a bit."

"Oh, Sam," Kylie breathed. She held her little sister close to her and felt her own heart breaking. She could feel that Sam was wearing only a bra and panties and shivering madly like she was in some kind of drug withdrawal. Kylie took off the ski jacket she'd been wearing when they'd thrown her in here and wrapped it around Sam. But she didn't know that it would help. Mac had said it looked like the girls were using drugs.

She swallowed dryly. *Mac had said.* Yes, he'd said and Kylie had believed. Was everything he'd told her lies? Was the way he'd looked at her? The possibility of that broke her heart and she clutched her baby sister tighter.

"But...but...I'm okay," Samantha said. "Ogano's dad, he's the president of this really big Japanese company. That's why they're all here, right? The Sato company is really really rich. So Ogano, he says...he says..."

Samantha seemed to lose her train of thought and Kylie told her it was okay and stroked her hair, long golden hair she'd envied as Sam had grown up and gotten the lion's share of their parents' attention. Or so it had seemed to Kylie at the time.

So what had been so lacking in Samantha's life that she could have fallen for someone like Tibor Balakirev?

And what had been so lacking in Kylie's own life that she'd fallen for Macaulay Rush?

She closed her eyes and wished beyond wishing that she was wrong in doubting him. And maybe Sam was wrong in doubting the good intentions of Ogano Sato too. Maybe his involvement in this gang of thugs was strictly familial and really did plan to rescue Samantha somehow.

As if reading her thoughts, Samantha suddenly jerked and said, "Ogano will rescue you too, of course. Yeah. We'll get out of here tomorrow, Kylie."

"Sure we will," Kylie said and resumed stroking Samantha's hair.

~~~~

"Where is *Sam?*" Ogano Sato roared, his face red and swollen with drink.

For just a moment, Tibor Balakirev, wished he had never

agreed with his partner's suggestion to contact a Yakuza family and bring them out here. Not that Tibor had compunctions about selling Samantha Michaelson to them, but one thing he had inherited from his father was a snobbery towards men who could not hold their vodka. And none of these Yakuza, except perhaps Hachiuma Sato himself, could drink more than ten shots of Moscovskaya without becoming foolish or belligerent.

Ogana was one of the belligerent ones.

Tibor flipped his hair back and stared imperiously down at the shorter man. Ogano looked like a wobbling potato, he thought, face mealy and dimpled, square body almost ready to topple. "Where," he asked, "is our agreed-upon payment?"

"Minute!" Ogano said and wobbled off to the side of the room. He pawed sloppily through a small bag he kept in the corner while Tibor watched with interest. Had the man actually brought cash to this upper room? Had any of the others, also?

Perhaps they had, Tibor thought. Perhaps they believed that the fierceness of their triple dragon tattoos, the top snouts of which just peaked up the back of their necks, or the horror of their missing digits—all but Ogano seemed to be missing at least one joint from their little fingers; others had lost as many as two whole fingers, which signaled some bad mistakes they'd felt compelled to apologize to their *Oyabun* for—protected them from being robbed. Or perhaps they assumed Tibor needed his deal with them badly enough that he would not dare.

Both assumptions were wrong. Despite his partner's insistence that they had to build this alliance, Tibor found he did not like these Japanese criminals. Hachiuma, in his fifties, was far too much like Tibor's own father, and assumed he would run any alliance. His underlings were uneducated pigs. Perhaps he would have Slava and Maksim search their rooms and persons before they left here tonight.

Still, if they could produce this much ready cash in one trip...

Ogano was stumbling back to him with a large manila envelope. He shoved it into Tibor's hands. "Count!" he ordered. "All there!"

Indeed? Tibor opened the envelope and pulled out a wad of the well-used, therefore likely untraceable, one hundred and five hundred dollar bills. American currency. Presumably it was the amount they had agreed on for Samantha Michaelson—$120,000.

Tibor was impressed. Just how much loose cash had the Sato clan carried here for the meeting?

Smiling tightly at Ogano, he said, "I will bring her out tomorrow morning."

"Now!"

"When she's had proper time to think and your father is ready to commit to a long-term alliance with us, on my terms," he said thickly. "Then I will bring her out to you. Then I will order her to do every little perverted act your porcine heart desires."

Ogano blinked stupidly at him. Tibor was sure he'd understood nothing of that. Nor was Tibor about to call over a girl to translate. Not yet. Not when he'd just seen his partner finally arrive for the tail end of this Monday-night *prazdnik na tri bukvy*, the "holiday from hell."

Ogano stuck out his lower lip. "Now?"

"Tomorrow," Tibor repeated.

He handed the manila envelope to Maksim to stow in the office while he, Tibor, walked to the door with his arms spread suddenly wide.

"John! Alyssa! Jerome! It is so good that you could make it to the party!"

~~~~

Mac stood in the parking garage across the street from where his floating house was anchored. In front of him, in Level 2, Stall B-45, sat a canvas-covered, uninsured luxury model BMW convertible that he used to drive like a muscle-brained maniac back in the days when he litigated day and night for a living.

Now he rode a snowboard and drove a motorcycle. Had he really changed?

Yes, he answered himself. Now all his speed and skill were devoted to achieving absolutely nothing. No fights, no taking on the big guys, defending the weak. Now he'd been reduced to helplessly talking some overworked police officer to boredom while two women at least, one of whom he'd nonverbally committed himself to, were trapped, and possibly in danger.

Should he jump in this car and go roaring up to Milaya Ridge?

He clenched his jaw in frustration, trying to imagine a scenario where that would help. All he came up with was closed doors and a blown cover. Assuming he hadn't already done that by opening up to John; he hoped he hadn't. To actually try a frontal assault on Tibor's rooms, though, could easily set off Tibor's unpredictable defense mechanisms. He might hurt Kylie, Samantha, or even *all* of the women he had there.

No. What Mac needed was a way to stall whatever deal Tibor was trying to push through, keep them all up there negotiating long enough for Mac to convince the police they needed to move in.

And suddenly he hit upon a way to do just that.

It would require a ton of hasty legal work, some hard phone

calls to call in favors, some judicious groveling and brilliant argument before a judge tomorrow morning.

The way, in other words, the legal game was played.

He hoped that this time he could make it work.

# 22

Tuesday morning at Milaya Ridge was one of those pristine mornings where the sky seemed to float its blue right up to space. No clouds, mist, or wind. A woman drinking a latte on their condo balcony in the Hillside pointed her partner's gaze to the top of Schlatter where the small dot of a snowmobile made its way over the hump to the helicopter pad on the mountain's east shoulder to prep the chopper for the day's use. The chairlifts were beginning their test runs. The first busses and cars were arriving in the parking lot.

For Kylie, however, there was nothing to signal the hour but her eyes blinking open. The room where she and Samantha were locked up let in only minimal light from the hallway. Just enough that when her eyes had finally adjusted last night, Samantha had looked like an apparition in the darkness, her long hair falling in dark shadows around her face, her body gaunt and hunched over under Kylie's jacket.

So it could have been four a.m. Six a.m.? That was her usual wake-up times. But she'd slept so poorly last night it could be noon for all she knew. Her bladder was full to bursting and her belly...

Kylie sniffed. She thought she smelled coffee from somewhere and it made her insides clench with hunger. Not helpful. She shook it off and concentrated. Were those sounds of conversation? There was also a slight hum in the floor like some sort of machinery had started up. Putting her ear to the dirty linoleum, she thought she could hear irregular thumping sounds. An early store employee awake down there? Someone who could free them?

"Sam," she whispered and nudged her sister, who was wheezing gently on top of Kylie's stomach, Kylie's jacket covering both of them.

Samantha had woken Kylie repeatedly last night when her bare legs had done some weird kicking motion, but now Baby Face wouldn't budge. Kylie remembered that behavior from when they'd both lived at home. Kylie would spring out of bed on Saturday mornings and be conscripted to clean house while precious little Samantha was allowed to snooze the entire morning away.

"Sam!" Kylie poked her hard.

Samantha started, grunted, and Kylie saw her lift her head, her face twisted enough in the pain of wakening that Kylie could just make it out. "Kylie?" she said.

"People are up. People downstairs. We need to get their attention."

So saying, she raised her right foot without getting up, and slammed it down on the floor. It made a dull whack and made her think of going pee again. Not *helpful*. She clenched hard and slammed her foot down again. And again. She brought the other foot into play until she was playing a kind of tattoo.

Samantha rolled up to her knees, holding the jacket around her, and started to giggle.

Kylie stopped, gripping her tummy. "What?" she snapped.

"You look like you're having a temper tantrum."

"Oh, that's helpful." Kylie rolled stiffly to her feet and stomped from a standing position. Again. Then she put her fists to her hips and stomped both feet, one after another. She looked over at Sam, holding a fist to her dark face, and snickered a bit herself. "No better, hunh?"

Samantha shook her face and giggled again.

"I have to pee."

"Me too," said Sam and they both giggled.

"Maybe I should yell and scream."

Samantha's giggling stopped and she shook her head. "Tibor doesn't like that. I did that once, my first day here, and..." She shut her mouth but Kylie could hear the fear.

"He hit you?"

She shook her head. "Slava. He got Slava to hit me on the bottom of my feet so there wouldn't be marks."

"Oh, Sam," Kylie said and walked to her sister, kneeling uncomfortably beside her and stroking her hair. How could she be jealous of her sister? Sam was just Sam. Kylie's issues were with her parents. They weren't Samantha's fault. Though how could Samantha had let herself get sucked into something so evil? Why couldn't she be more like Kylie? Strong. Kylie might sleep with a man the first day she met him...and the second day, but she never let him lead her into captivity.

No, Kylie had managed to lead her*self* into it.

Still, if she'd gotten herself into this, she was also going to get herself and Samantha out of it. She just had to think. *Think.* An empty room. One locked door. The two of them in here.

"Sam, listen," she said. "First we're going to use that corner over there to relieve ourselves, then this is what we do."

~~~~

Judge Marilyn Waters looked up from the thick sheaf of papers in front of her to fix her narrow eyed glance squarely on Mac.

He stood neatly attired in his best navy suit, the closet dust hurriedly brushed off before he'd rushed out at seven this morning to meet with his new clients. And even though this was insanity—the all night research and materials prep, the late phone calls, the explanations, the expedited reinstatement of his practice insurance so he could appear here now—he felt good. Like he almost knew this job. Like he'd never left.

Deep down that terrified him, but that was an emotion he was *not* going to show.

The judge suddenly cracked a smile. "Good to see you back, Mr. Rush."

"Thank you, Milady."

"This request for a Mareva injunction and Anton Pillar action..." She fingered the two inches of material. They contained his all night effort redrafted and bound together with Milaya company statements; stuff from Leonid Balakirev and Mac's new clients, Evergreen Holdings, that set out the believed state of Tibor's financial affairs; and an admittedly shaky affidavit from the receptionist at Milaya Resorts whom he'd had to coach and get a signature from via fax. "It's unusual."

"Yes, Milady." Mac could feel the frowns of Evergreen's CFO behind him. Mac had assured them this was a necessary move, and a sure thing at that. They would freeze all of Tibor's assets until an application for a declaration of his bankruptcy could be filed.

"But if you'll turn to page four, where I set out the need for an expedited order..."

~~~~

Samantha let out a bloodcurdling scream. In the dark center of the room, *wearing* Kylie's ski jacket now, she dropped her head down for breath, then drew it back up and screamed again.

Kylie watched in awe from her position beside the door, forcing herself not to cover her ears. She'd never have believed Baby Face had it in her; she'd always seemed a lightweight. Then again, all this stuff Samantha had been through had to have been terrifying. Maybe it had forced her to grow up a little.

And Kylie? Was there anything that would ever force *her* to grow up, to get over herself? Being reduced to peeing on the floor in the corner had been close, but not quite there. Maybe seeing Mac hurt? Or finding out that he was really one of the bad guys, in league with Tibor after all?

Yes, that sort of betrayal would do something.

Her right fist tightened around the screw-in end of the light bulb she and Samantha had managed to get down from the ceiling. They'd smashed it carefully against the floor in the corner and now Kylie held it as a weapon. She was desperate enough, and cranky enough from lack of food, that she thought she could use it.

As Sam drew herself up for a fourth scream, Kylie held up her hand. She heard someone coming.

The footsteps paused outside the door and a hand fumbled

with the useless light switch, then with the door lock. Kylie signaled Samantha to get ready. Baby Face let loose just as the door swung inward.

The figure of John Rush, backlit by the blinding light of hallway startled Kylie but not enough to stop her fist holding the light bulb from smashing hard against his face, spinning him sideways with Kylie following him down as he fell.

She'd put everything she had into that and her right hand felt broken, an explosion of pain, but the man was down! She turned her fist to point the jagged end of the broken bulb at Rush's neck, willing him to open his eyes and *see* it.

Samantha screeched again and Kylie was suddenly grabbed from behind, lifted bodily off Mac's brother like she weighed nothing, her right hand smashed against the doorframe so she dropped the broken bulb. Kylie had a quick impression of a short beard, an ill-fitting suit.

Slava! Why couldn't it have been Maksim?

The Russian bodyguard shoved her up against the inside wall beside the door and drew back a meaty hand to slap her, when John Rush lifted a hand and croaked, "Stop. She's mine."

Slava looked at Kylie, sniffed, and wrinkled his nose at the stink of the room, but he stayed his hand.

John Rush picked himself up from the floor and limped over to her with a twisted grin. He waved off the Russian, who looked uncertain for a moment, then he stooped to pick up the broken light bulb and stepped out into the hall. John closed the door behind him.

He turned to Kylie and Sam.

What would he do now? Punish them? Rape them? For all that she'd been shaken up, Kylie's blood was boiling. Every self-defense class she'd ever taken was spilling through her head and she was unconsciously forming her hands into jabbing weapons. The eyes. The bridge of the nose. She slid away from the wall in a bouncing little dance around Rush. He wasn't going to take her without a fight.

But Rush didn't move towards her. Instead he looked at Samantha. "Make slapping sounds and grunts. Cry out like you're getting beaten. I need to talk to your sister."

Without waiting for Samantha to comply or for Kylie to figure this out, he began talking quickly. "Okay, look. I just found out about you and your sister here this morning. You're part of this...deal that Tibor's cooked up with the Japanese guys."

"The Yakuza."

"Apparently," said John. He reminded Kylie a little of Macaulay in the wry way he spoke and stood, as if he believed in himself completely, but wasn't too sure about everything else. The quick gestures though were more nervous, less focused than Mac's. They didn't inspire the same level of trust.

"Anyway, the upshot is this. Ogano has bought your sister here for $120,000 U.S. funds. He plans to take her back to Japan as his personal property."

Samantha suddenly slapped a wall hard with her hands and cried out. Again. Kylie heard the real pain.

"Tibor figured he'd use you to make sure she complied, then kill you."

More slapping and grunting.

"But somehow Ogano's father, Hachiuma, the leader of the whole group, the one Tibor's trying to cut the deal with, got wind that Tibor had you captured here too. He offered $200,000 and an alliance agreement if you were thrown into the deal."

"What?!" Kylie said.

"Apparently Maruyama, the guy who rescued you from the snowstorm yesterday, couldn't stop talking about you. Hachiuma was sizing you up at the party last night. Then the way you got Mac to come to me, asking questions, the way you fought back against Slava when he and Bo grabbed you downtown. Hachiuma somehow knows all this and likes it. I think he sees you as a wild horse he wants to tame."

Kylie reeled. She was being...*bought?* Like an animal. Like a common prostitute. Like one of Tibor's girls. And here she'd been so smug about how any of them would have let themselves get into this situation.

John had stopped talking and Samantha had stopped hitting the wall and crying out. There was the sound of a hand on the doorknob and Sam quickly began hitting the wall and grunting again.

Kylie took a deep breath and faced John, who seemed to be waiting for something. "You're going to help us," she said.

"I want to." He was listening to her keenly, as if he was used to taking orders from older women. Like Alyssa, of course.

"When are they going to come for us?" Kylie asked.

John shook his head. "Tibor didn't say."

"Can you distract them then come let us out?"

He shook again. "I'm watched too closely. He even finds out I've talked to you like this, he'll kill me. Or get Slava to." He looked nervously back towards the door.

"Police?"

"He'd just move you sooner."

Samantha slapped the wall, moaned, then came running over to John, throwing her arms around him in such an overtly sexual way that Kylie stepped back in disgust. "You have to get us out," Sam cooed into his ear and stroked his hair. "We'll be ever so grateful."

"Get off me," he said through clenched teeth and peeled her arms from around his neck, forcing her back. "I can't *do* anything."

The doorknob was turning and Sam threw herself dramatically to the ground. But Kylie stepped closer to John so that even in this dimmest of light, she could look square into his face. "Listen," she hissed. "You slap me when that door opens, then laugh, strut out of here, and find a way to call your brother."

"Mac?"

"Mac." Her stomach grumbled. "And get us some food."

# 23

"THEY HAVE DONE WHAT?" said Tibor.

"Slapped an injunction on you," said his partner. "That means you can't move any assets out of the country. They'll be watching your usual transport trucks. Do you suppose someone knows you're planning to sell off your livestock?"

Tibor spun, his face cold but prickling with color in the cheeks. "This means nothing. I will move no money out, no trucks. And if people leave, so what? They do not have a right to stop my guests from coming and going as they please."

The partner gave a head shake. "You don't get it. There's an Anton Pillar order as well for production of all your financial records. It's a lawyer's ruse. Macaulay Rush, somehow. It's a way to let the police search the place, check anything moving in and out of here. My guess is you'll have at least two RCMP cars up here checking things out by this afternoon."

"Then we move the two girls earlier."

"If you're prepared to cut short Hachiuma's final day of skiing. But you still haven't told me how you'll get the sisters on a commercial flight back to Japan. The younger one might cooperate with the other as hostage. But getting the old one on? Uh-unh. She's a fighter."

Tibor shook his head and smiled. Here was one thing at least that he had managed to arrange without consulting his partner. And he believed the solution was brilliant. He implied as much as he flipped back his long hair and described the plan.

When he was done, the partner nodded. "Until then we keep those two girls locked up tight. No one sees them or speaks to them."

"The other girls?"

The partner snorted. "Most are on the hills. The others don't matter. As long as Hachiuma and son are happy, we have a deal and the beginning of an empire."

~~~~

By twelve-thirty, Mac had not only had his injunction and Anton Pillar, he'd also spent nearly an hour and a half with the province's RCMP and Vancouver's police department, furiously arguing they had to move sooner than later on Milaya Ridge. The original detective who'd questioned him about his motorbike accident and its connection to Jackson Pollard's death surprisingly chipped in on Mac's side.

But when it was clear that any movement was still going to take at least an hour or two, Mac stormed out, jogged around the corner to where he'd discretely parked his BMW, and blasted up the Sea-to-Sky highway to Milaya Ridge.

Why he felt this sudden, overwhelming urgency about rescuing Kylie he couldn't have said. The fact they'd kidnaped her this time rather than try to run her down again suggested they'd changed their minds about killing her. Maybe the buzz after Jackson Pollard's death had made them nervous. Maybe John told them Mac had gone to the police.

Still, something in Mac's gut told him time was running out. Call it a psychic connection or a lover's worry, he didn't care. He just knew he had to save her from Tibor *now*.

A police car slowed his progress near the Milaya Ridge cut-off, but once he made that and got onto the winding road climbing steeply into the mountains, Mac floored the gas pedal. He almost lost it twice on sharp turns and had to slow down once the roads took on a permanent base of snow.

He still made Milaya Ridge in under seventy minutes. Roaring into the parking lot half-expecting to see Slava or Maksim loading Kylie, bound and gagged, into the back of a truck beside her sister.

Instead he saw a full lot. He drove around twice before taking a spot where someone pulled out. Then he sat there in a cold sweat, his heart pumping hard, his hands gripping the steering wheel, and thought, *Now what?*

He was dressed in a twelve hundred dollar suit and wingtip shoes. A fish out of water up here. Ridiculous. And he had nowhere to go anyway. How was he supposed to carry out his bold rescue? March up to Tibor's herringbone door, bang on it loudly, and demand entrance?

Maybe he could tell him that his daddy was very displeased with him. Yeah, that would work. Tell him his daddy basically wanted to shut down his whole operation, so could Tibor just be a good son and give up?

"Cripes," he said and banged his head back against his headrest. What now? What...now?

It would be so easy to just sit there and wait for the cops, or even turn around? Leave? He'd gotten the cops to come up here at least. He'd started a lawsuit that should bring Tibor down even if they couldn't arrest him for kidnaping.

Right. Like this clenching in his gut would let him drive away? If Kylie was being hurt...

The next second he was out of his car, slamming and locking the door, and setting off, slipping and sliding in his smooth-soled shoes, for the Lodge. Rather than go in, though, he cut around the outside to the right. The ski and snowboard rental building was about fifteen yards southeast of the front entrance. It was also where he'd picked up his students the two weeks he'd been teaching here. They knew him. That had to count for something.

It did. Joey, after laughing his ass off over Mac's appearance, pulled him into the back room where all the skis, boards, and boots where. There he grabbed the purple snow pants he'd probably been planning on wearing later that afternoon. He literally loaned Mac the matching ski jacket off his back.

"Think of it as a trade, dude," he said, and, as Mac took off his own tailor-made suit jacket, Joey grabbed it and slipped it on.

"You have any idea how much that costs?" Mac said.

"Hey, you let me wear the whole outfit for a few hours to impress the babes and I'll throw in a board, boots, and my day pass. Very clean."

Mac laughed and began tugging off his shirt and tie. He was down to his sock feet on the rubber matting and pulling on Joey's pants, when the cell phone he'd pulled out with his wallet and keys started chiming.

He finished tugging on the pants and grabbed it, answered. "Yo?"

John's voice whispered, "Mac, listen. Tibor's just headed out to find Hachiuma on the hills. You remember him?"

"Head of the Yakuza. The guy I guided down the hill yesterday." Joey raised his eyebrows at him from where he was clumsily knotting Mac's tie around his own neck. Mac stepped into the very back of the room, in between the skis and cupped his hand around the mouth of the cell phone.

"Tibor's got a deal going with him," John rushed on. "His son's bought Kylie's little sister. Hachiuma's purchased Kylie. They're getting them out this afternoon."

Mac's whole body flushed cold. "How?"

"I don't know! I'm not privy to that. I wasn't supposed to know *any* of this except I heard Jerome laughing about it this morning."

"Jerome?"

There was an embarrassed pause on the connection. "I brokered this deal, but when Jerome found out, he wanted in. He decided it was something the entire firm had to get behind. Big new client. I think he plans to retire on it."

"Which is why you'll be moving to his office."

"I swear to God, Mac, that I had no idea about these girls."

"Or the murder."

"Or the murder. And I was going to try to work something out, but Kylie..."

Mac jerked. "What about her? Is she alright?"

"She's fine. She's... Goddammit, bro'. You like strong women."

"And you don't get this one. Where's Tibor holding her?"

"In one of these upper rooms. That's where we're all camped out. It's like a frigging war room up here. Maksim and Slava guarding the doors. Everyone huddling and planning. That injunction thing, by the way. That was you?"

"Guilty."

"Stupid. It's got them scared. Everything's going down faster now. Soon as Tibor gets Hachiuma off Schlatter, Kylie and sister are gone."

Joey called to Mac and, when Mac turned, struck a model's pose in Mac's suit. Not a bad fit, but Joey had slightly narrower shoulders and slimmer hips so the suit hung a bit loose. He'd look really graceful in those shoes the first time he stepped out into the snow to help someone adjust their bindings.

Mac turned back to the phone. "So how are we going to get them out?"

"I don't know." Mac could almost see John tossing up his free hand. "Hey, you're the chess player who could beat Dad. You're the golden boy. I'm just the corporate guy."

"Oh, stuff it. Look, has anyone mentioned a truck, car, the limo?"

"I don't know. But there's only the one road in or out, right?"

"Yes," said Mac, thinking furiously, "but it's going to be blocked by cops before..." He trailed off. He suddenly knew how Tibor could get the girls out. And before he could discount it as too daring for the younger Balakirev, it suddenly clicked with something Leonid had mentioned yesterday.

Everything clicked. Horribly.

"John, Tibor's not there right now. Right?"

"Right." He heard the caution in the voice.

"Okay, then listen. Here's what I want you to do."

~~~~

When John beeped off his phone and slid it back into the pocket of his corduroys, he felt sick.

Mac didn't know what he was asking. Or, well, yes, he probably did. But it was easy enough for him. He'd already shot his life all to pieces. He didn't really have anything left to lose, did he?

But John, he had everything to lose. He had his dream, his future as a rich, successful corporate lawyer. If he did what Mac asked, everything about Milaya Ridge would come out. All the questionable financing, the doctored accounting he'd arranged in order to land at least three of their current investors. They were talking tens of millions of dollars here. It wasn't something corporate types just wrote off, especially in Canada.

And now Tibor had gone hip deep into criminality. Murder? Yakuza? What was he thinking? Or had John just been willfully blind this whole time he'd been structuring Tibor's deals?

Yes, willfully blinded by the money. The payoff. But—

"Johnny? What are you doing here in the dark?"

John jerked around as the door to the bedroom where he and Alyssa had stayed last night cracked open. Alyssa poked in her head. Backlit by the smoky light of Tibor's main upper room, all the wrinkles around her eyes seemed deeper. But her wasp-thin figure, always an attraction for him and even more when she was dressed in a skin-tight sweater and slacks now, seemed to lean almost seductively against the doorframe. As if the hustle and buzz of Tibor's planning excited her and she wanted a quickie right then and there.

John swallowed dryly. Oh, to be able to just grab her and ravish her the way he'd done that first time he'd stayed over at Mac's for Christmas. She'd invited him. She'd led him on with glances and "accidental" touches.

And every time he'd scored big after that—his position with Rapney, Smythe & Walker; his first independently handled corporate merger—she'd visited him again to celebrate.

John had been truly sorry when Mac's life had fallen apart for him, and sorrier still when Alyssa had walked out, but John had understood. Alyssa needed a man with *cojones*. She needed money and power. And because John had been able to give her that, it seemed only natural that John take up where his big brother had failed.

Until now.

Now, with what Mac wanted him to help do.

"I'm just thinking," he lied to Alyssa. "I'm contemplating how sweet our life is going to be when Milaya is fully developed and the money starts rolling in. It'll be bigger than Intrawest."

The words stuck in his throat. Even more as he saw her smile and slip into the room with him, wrap her arms around him in that way she had, her long fingers running up his spine to the back of his head and twirling his hair. He could feel her hot body against his, her groin pressing into him, urging him back towards the bed.

And he could take her. She was his. All his. Forever. All he had to do was nothing at all. One final betrayal of his brother.

"Let's shut the door," he said thickly.

# 24

MAC'S MIND WAS IN OVERDRIVE MODE as he carried his snowboard out across the front of the ski lodge and headed for the base of Schlatter.

Everything had gone as cold and clear for him as the mountain skies today. Tibor was at Schlatter to get Hachiuma Sato. Skiing or simply waiting at the lift, Mac couldn't be sure. Either way, Mac had to get to Tibor first. Then he'd start with a bluff—call it an initial negotiating position—that he had the full financial goods on Tibor from John, that he could pull the plug with all of Tibor's investors tomorrow, *and* permanently scuttle Tibor's development applications working their way through government, unless Tibor was willing to deal.

Failing that, he'd promise to retract evidence he'd given police.

If Tibor still didn't budge, Mac would subdue him by force and use physical pain to make him take Mac to Kylie. "Last refuge of the weak mind," his father would have called this tactic. Then again, the old man never countenanced his love of fast cars or motorcycles either.

There was a good five minute line-up at the bottom of

Schlatter, even with it being a state of the art quad chairlift. Tibor was nowhere in sight.

Mac sucked in the thrum of lift, the skritch of skiers and boarders turning to stop at the bottom and slide into the lineup. If this had been even two days ago, before Kylie, Mac would have put everything about Tibor and Leonid aside and just ridden the chair up to get in touch with snow and sky.

Feed my soul. Set me free.

He felt the slightest tinge of regret that his brief idle in the carefree life had come to an end two nights ago. Kind of like that moment, teetering at the top of a run before you committed your soul to the downhill rush.

Now it was time for him to commit. He tossed his borrowed board down onto the snow and slammed his left boot into the front binding. Joey rode regular, rather than goofy. It felt strange, but Mac could ride either way. And all he really cared about right now was finding Tibor.

But as he used his rear foot to push himself up the little slope to the instructor's line of the lift, he heard his name being gruffly called.

Turning, he saw three skiers poling vigorously toward him. In the lead, the one who'd called to him, was the short blunt figure of Hachiuma Sato. Just off his left arm, poling effortlessly to keep up, was the same redheaded escort he'd had during the blizzard when Mac had first met the two of them and guided them down the hill.

Behind them, his long black hair flapping lightly as he poled to catch up, was the tall, thin figure of Tibor Balakirev.

"Rush-san. Wait," Sato ordered Mac, though Mac had already stopped and clicked out of his front binding.

The trio stopped. Sato gave a little bow, showing Mac far more respect than he had that day on the hill. Then, before Tibor could say anything, Sato had used his poles to stab the release button on the rear of his bindings and step out of his skis. He muttered something to the redhead in Japanese, and she said to Mac, "Mr. Sato would like you to accompany us back to the lodge."

Tibor slid forward on is skis to block Mac's way. "Maybe that is not a good idea," he said, trying his best to burn Mac into submission with his gaze.

Mac laughed. "I think it's a great idea. Though," he addressed the redhead, "I have to confess I'm a little bit puzzled as to why Mr. Sato wants me to accompany him. My understanding is that he's recently purchased a woman I think I'm in love with."

The redhead blinked, visibly taken aback. She looked to Tibor's fixed, furious face, then to Hachiuma Sato. "Um...uh..."

"Go ahead and translate," Mac said.

Sato held up a gloved hand. "No need. I understand very completely."

Mac saw the shock flash across Tibor's face before the Russian stowed it beneath a scowl. So, everyone in this little negotiation had their secrets.

"Mr. Rush-san," Sato said. "I feeling very bad for taking your woman today."

"So nice to hear that," Mac said.

"This way of world, yes? Strong always take pick."

"It would seem."

"But strong is also be generous."

"You're going to give her back? Maybe her sister too?"

Sato's hard old mouth twitched, like he appreciated the joke. He shook his head. "I give you goodbye. You come to room. You say goodbye, *hai*? Last goodbye. Gift for you save my life on hill."

Mac's smile pulled back tautly as he thought of a dozen answers to that. Finally he just shot a disgusted look at Tibor and nodded. "*Hai*," he said.

~~~~

There was a rattling sound and tromping feet outside the door of the bare room where Kylie and Samantha waited.

Why did it have to sound so much like prison guards coming to take them to the electric chair?

She waited tensely, holding Samantha's hand, but when the door opened and the blinding light of the hallways made both of them cover their eyes, no one rushed in to get them. Nor were there a group of guards. Just two. The one in front, Kylie saw when her vision had finally adjusted to the light, was one of Tibor's girls, Galette, the one who'd saved her on the ski hill.

She gave Kylie a quick smile and winked at Samantha. Then she pushed a serving cart in ahead of her, stopped, and took from its bottom shelf what looked like a large bucket of steaming water, two toothbrushes, a tube of toothpaste, and a bar of soap.

From the top shelf she lifted off two steaming cups and two covered plates. All their smells hit Kylie at once like a warm slap. Some kind of tea! Bacon! Fruit? Eggs maybe?

Kylie was about to lunge for the plates when Galette, who'd stepped quickly back with the now-empty cart, moved to one side to let the second visitor step in.

Slava.

He lumbered forward like he wanted to rush Kylie and snap her in two. But he stopped, lifted up a short dress he had slung over his left arm, and tossed it at Samantha. He grabbed a second dress from his left arm and tossed a similar dress at Kylie. "After you eat, you wash up, you put on these clothes," he said.

Faint with the desire for food, Kylie nonetheless crossed her arms over her chest and laughed. "Or what?"

Slava rocked forward on his toes. "Or I," he said slowly, drawing out each word like he was pushing it out through his nose, "will come in and make you do it. I'd like that."

Unlike the stoically grumpy way Maksim had taken Mac's sassing the other night, this Russian looked like he'd happily forget any orders he'd had about not touching the merchandise.

Still Kylie couldn't help saying, "In your dreams, bub."

Slava stalked forward and Kylie hastily backed away, right to the wall, but Slava kept coming. Desperately, she lunged to the corner she and Samantha had used to relieve themselves earlier and crouched down beside it, holding out her hand like a scoop.

"Come closer," she said to the Russian. "Come on."

Slava stopped, his nose wrinkling back again, and he pointed his finger at her. "Soon," he said.

Kylie kept her mouth shut this time and Slava finally backed up, turned on his heel, and left the room, slamming the door behind him and plunging the room back into darkness.

Kylie carefully eased herself away from the stench of the corner, gagging, and crept to the middle of the room to find Samantha collapsed there and crying softly.

When Kylie touched her, Sam's whole body shuddered and she said, "I'm sorry, Ky. I'm so sorry. I'm stupid. I'm sorry."

Kylie felt her own eyes watering and she swallowed hard. "Samantha, if anyone should be sorry it's me. I left you alone back in Madison."

"I...I had Mom and Dad."

"But I should have been there more. At least called. Been a big sister."

Samantha said nothing and that made the pain in Kylie's chest even sharper.

"But you know what? I think I'm finally able to do that. As soon as we get out of here—"

"We're not getting out of here!" Samantha cried. "Except as slaves! Have you seen what these Japanese hoods do to them*selves*? All these cut off little fingers! These weird body piercings and tattoos! What do you think they'll do to us?! What do you think—"

"Stop!" Kylie shook Sam's shoulder hard. "We will get out of here. We've got John Rush working with us on the inside. We've got his brother, Macaulay, working for us on the outside. Mac will have police, army guys, whatever it takes. Believe me, Samantha! We're getting free very soon."

Samantha's body was shaking and quivering now and Kylie wondered how much of it was from fear, how much from drug withdrawal.

"Either way," Kylie told her gently, "we need to eat. And getting washed up, at least, sounds good, right?"

Sam shivered again but nodded weakly.

"Then let's do it. Have to be ready for our big break."

She urged Samantha over to the food and they carefully fumbled up their cups of tea in the near blackness. They went for the food next.

While Kylie's brain started a running patter of, *Come on, Mac. Where are you? Come on.*

~~~~

One turn of the hallway over, through a door into Tibor's great room, across it and behind a closed and locked door, John Rush fell back on his guest bed's pillow and gazed up at Alyssa with glazed eyes.

She sat straddling him, gazing off into space as she brushed out her hair with her fingers. She looked bored.

But John didn't mind. Alyssa hadn't been that energetic with him since almost the first night they were together. It had to be the excitement of the deal. The idea that they were this close to securing all the money for Milaya that they'd ever need.

Had Alyssa accepted that these Japanese "investors" weren't strictly legit? All the tense discussions out there between John, Tibor, Jerome about the state of negotiations were done using code words. The whole picture had only fully made sense to John himself once he accepted Mac's claim that Sato and company were Yakuza. Had Jerome known that already? And Alyssa had heard that claim. Did she disbelieve it because it came from Mac? Or did she believe it and just not care?

Just as it occurred to John that maybe this ought to worry him, Alyssa dropped her body forward onto him and stretched his arms up over his head.

"Shall I tie you to the bed, lover?" she crooned into his ear. "Ready for another round?"

John jerked down his arms and pushed her off him, suddenly remembering his promise to Mac. His *broken* promise, one he couldn't possibly fulfill. Still... "No. We have to get out there. I have to get out there. When Tibor comes back with Sato, that's the key. Deal time. If I'm not there, Jerome will claim it was all him. He'll try to cut us out."

Alyssa popped off the bed and began pulling on her clothes. "Well I was starting to wonder if you cared."

He looked at her sharply. "Meaning what?"

"Oh, nothing, darling. Nothing at all."

Feeling a yet another knot of discomfort join the ones already coiling in his stomach, John went for his clothes too.

He was just zipping his suit pants when a great thumping and mumbling from the main room announced the arrival of a group of people. John stuffed his shirt into his pants, grabbed his tie, and began doing a half-Windsor when a voice suddenly rose above the others.

It was Mac. And he sounded angry.

# 25

"KYLIE!" Mac shouted a second time, and pushed away Tibor when he stepped up angrily. "John!"

This second name made Tibor snap back his head in surprise and turn to Mac's right. Following the glance, Mac saw Jerome Smythe shrugging his shoulders and rising from one of the room's great overstuffed armchairs.

"Should have known you'd be here," Mac said to him. "You're a disgrace to the legal profession."

"Now now, Gunner," said Smythe. "I've heard you're getting back into law. Don't say things you'll regret later."

"You want to know my one regret, you sonofabitch?" He clenched his fists and stepped towards Smythe.

From the far side of the room, Slava stepped away from his guard duty in front of a door. But before he took a second step, Hachiuma Sato was suddenly in front of Mac. The Yakuza's short square body stood very still. His eyes glittered.

"You are upset," Sato said. His tone said it was Mac's one chance to backpedal.

"Just want my goodbye kiss," Mac said, and did a little

pirouette with a foolish grin. He threw his arms wide. "Kylie!"

It was a calculated cockiness, only half in control. Because besides himself, Smythe, Sato, Galette, and Slava, the great room was deserted. John wasn't there. Kylie wasn't there. The other Yakuza and their dates weren't there. Which meant Mac's idea for breaking Kylie out of here, which depended on a certain level of random chaos, was going to fail unless Mac stirred things up a bit. It was like the cross-examination of a tough expert—you had to get things off balance and look for an opening.

The door behind him opened and Mac spun around.

John stumbled out, looking flushed, still straightening his tie. Alyssa walked casually out behind him. Even through the lingering smells of spilt alcohol and food in the room, the unmistakable scent of Alyssa's sex cut straight to Mac's nose.

It knocked him off-balance for a second. John, his brother, who'd called him, who'd promised help, was again betraying him with Alyssa. He'd taken her first when Mac had needed her most. Now he was fooling with her when Mac needed *John* most.

"What were you doing?" asked Tibor and something in his voice made Mac turn to him. That look in the young Balakirev's eyes, the way they flashed from John to Alyssa and back, Alyssa's casual ignorance of it.

Mac smiled. Too perfect. Alyssa was fooling around with Tibor.

"Yes, John, my brother," Mac said. "What *were* you and your *wife* doing alone together in that hot, sweaty room right now?"

John, looking like a deer caught in headlights, looked back and forth between Mac and Tibor. "Wh-what?"

"And, Alyssa," Mac continued, "how many times have you been up here when it's been just you and Tibor...and that room?"

On that, both Sato and Smythe turned to look at Tibor, who glared at Mac and over Mac's shoulder at Slava, no doubt wishing he could crush Mac now, even with all these witnesses watching.

But it was Alyssa's reaction that Mac truly won, for she flushed a deep crimson, something he'd never seen her do in his eight years of marriage to her. John caught it too and pulled the same stupefied blinking routine he'd done over word Yakuza yesterday in his office. "Allie?" he pleaded.

"*Otmudohat*," Tibor growled and Slava began coming across the room for Mac.

"Don't forget Daddy," Mac snapped at Tibor and Tibor held up his hand.

"Meaning what?" Tibor said.

"Meaning he sent me and watches over me." It was truth as springboard into fiction, with Mac trying to spin it out faster than they could shoot him down. "He's already contacted the one Sato calls *Oyabun*. This deal's a no go from the get go."

Now Tibor spun to Sato and the old man's frown trenched either side of his face. Whether it was anger at the lie or puzzlement, Mac would never find out, because at the moment, upstairs door of the inner room thumped and the hulking figure of Maksim led in a younger Yakuza whose flaccid resemblance to the older Sato pegged him as the son.

"Where—is—Sam!" he bellowed.

Sato snapped something at him too fast for Mac to follow, but it only enraged the younger man. He shoved his hands into the inner lining of his ski jacket and came out with a handgun, a big, dull-black honker that Mac couldn't imagine he'd brought over on the plane.

The electricity in the room shot up. The criminal types froze,

Galette screamed, Maksim lunged forward to grab Sato Jr. and got a backwards elbow to the gut when Sato Jr. suddenly showed off what a squat, flaccid little Yakuza with martial arts training could do.

Maksim stumble sideways.

Slava charged.

Sato Jr. coldly aimed and fired at Slava, catching him in the left upper chest, spinning the big man so he fell onto his other shoulder with a loud grunt of pain.

Maksim had regained his feet and was about to charge but Tibor barked an order and he stopped. Then Tibor held up his hands to Sato Jr.. "Ogano! It's okay. Sam is okay. Tell him, Galette."

Sato Jr.'s command of English obviously wasn't up to his father's but he seemed to hear the "okay" as he swung his gun from Jerome Smythe, to Mac, to Tibor, Maksim, Alyssa, John, back to Slava, groaning on the floor.

"No," Mac said suddenly. "He's lying. Samantha is dead. Tibor killed her. Translate that, Galette."

"*Nyet!*" snapped Tibor.

Sato Jr. spun towards Mac. Galette, eyes wide, opened and shut her mouth. Then Sato Jr. barked at her in Japanese and she spoke back just as quickly.

Now Sato Jr.'s gun spun towards Tibor and he took two quick steps that way, snapping his gun sight sideways at Maksim when the big man looked like he was going to move.

"You kill?" Sato Jr. said, pushing the gun barrel at Tibor's face. His eyes had the same glitter Mac had seen earlier in the father, but with none of the control.

"Maksim," Tibor said. "Get the sisters. Galette, tell him what we're doing."

~~~~

In their dark room in the back hall, Kylie and Samantha had heard the sounds of shouting, then a gunshot.

It had startled both of them up from their almost excessive clothes and hair straightening and made them run to the door, trying to hear more.

*Mac!* Kylie thought and pressed her ear to the wood. That had to be Mac's voice. But who had been shot? She felt a crushing sense of darkness trying to tumble in on her. She pushed it back furiously.

After they'd both eaten, Sam had shakingly stripped down, bathed, and put on the ordered dress, hysterically refusing to don Kylie's boots or ski jacket as well.

So Kylie, after she'd washed as best she could, put back on Alyssa's old jeans and Kylie's own blouse and ski jacket and boots. And just let Slava try to make her change. If she was being sold, she was sure the buyer wouldn't want her covered in bruises and scratches. The big Russian had to know that.

She hoped.

"Kylie?" Samantha whispered.

"Sh."

There were heavy footsteps. Slava. Oh, no. She stepped back from the door, pulling Sam with her. "Let me do the talking," she said.

The doorknob jiggled, the lock scraped, and the door opened. As Kylie and Sam squinted and blinked hard to shield her eyes from the light, the blocky form of the Russian resolved itself into...

"Maksim!"

The big man nodded. "Come. Tibor wants you."

"To sell us," Kylie pleaded. "To a bunch of Japanese gangsters who cut off their own fingers and tattoo their whole bodies."

The Russian set his chin, but Kylie saw him looking over Samantha's rocky appearance and sniffing the primitive state of their prison. "Come."

"Alright, Maksim," Kylie said. "Okay. Okay. Come on, Sis."

She pulled Samantha's arm up around her own shoulders so that Samantha had to put little weight on her feet. The bruises from Sam's beating there were mostly gone, but Sam still took the hint and walked like it was agony to do so.

Out of the corner of her eye, she saw Maksim frown as they limped past.

~~~~

The people in the great room had shifted. Ogano Sato had backed Tibor to the wall by the door, Galette beside him, facing the far door where Maksim had left to get Kylie and Samantha.

This way Ogano could keep all the others in sight in case any of them tried to do something stupid.

Mac wondered if that included Ogano's father. The steely-haired Yakuza boss stood very still and calm where he'd stood earlier beside Mac, as if making the point he would move only when there was a good reason to do so. Of all the people in the room, he seemed the least ruffled by his son's sudden violence.

Maybe that's because it was typical in Yakuza monthly meetings, what with chopped off fingers being ways to say you're sorry.

Mac himself had tried to fade back towards John, but had

been intercepted by Jerome Smythe. The old defense lawyer had crossed the room almost as casually as Sato Sr. stood in its center, and stopped Mac with a touch.

"Still stirring things up," he murmured quietly.

"And you're still sucking up to the money," Mac shot back.

"You have no idea how much. You think thirty percent of a two million dollar case is a big score. But this deal, Mac, when it goes through, when Tibor gets all his permits and backing—do you have any idea how many millions a year will go through Milaya Ridge?"

"No," said Mac quietly, his eyes flitting to John, who seemed torn between wanting to grill his wife about Tibor and hear what Smythe was saying to Mac. "But I get the feeling you're going to tell me."

"I'd love to. I'd even be prepared to cut you in for a little cooperation."

Mac raised his eyebrows. "What do you think I have to bargain with?"

"Leonid Balakirev. Is he really set to ruin his son?"

"It's already underway."

"But you could stop it."

It wasn't a question. Mac's mind boggled at the power Smythe thought he had. "Jerome," he said, "the police are already on their way here. The deal's dead. Anyone implicated in it is probably going to jail."

Smythe shook his head, his wrinkled mouth crinkling up. "Come on, Gunner. You're bluffing again. You got one injunction, a few financials. Together we could make this go away."

"It's gone way beyond that," Mac said.

The door on the far wall opened and Maksim pushed Kylie and her sister into the room.

~~~~

Kylie stumbled to a halt and felt her heart jump to her throat. Mac! He was there, not fifteen feet from her, in unfamiliar purple snow gear that looked tight on him. But when his gaze met hers, it locked hard. Trying to tell her something? That he had a plan? That he didn't?

Where was that psychic connection all the mushy hearts talked about when you needed it?

Or, Kylie thought desperately as her eyes flicked around the Tibor's large party room, was Mac not here for a rescue, but a send-off? Hachiuma Sato waited in the middle of the room like a bridegroom. In front of him, holding a gun to Tibor and his downed Russian muscle, Slava, stood a pig-like man whose face only gradually started looking familiar. He was a bad rendition of Hachiuma. He had to be the son, Ogano Sato.

He confirmed it when he held out his free left hand now, beckoning Samantha. "Here," he ordered.

Sam, sniffing and shooting a terrified plea to Kylie, walked in her bare feet around the still figure of Slava on the ground until she stood just in front of the younger Sato.

The younger Sato said something in Japanese to Galette, who hung by his right arm, and Galette drawled in pure Bronx, "He's demanding youse get his woman some boots for her feet."

"John," Tibor said in his heaviest Russian accent. "Go to the fireplace. Maybe some of the boots there will fit Miss Michaelson."

Kylie saw Mac and John exchange a look as John walked. The old lawyer from John's office Mac seemed to catch it and he stepped away from Mac.

Ogano turned to glance at the fireplace.

Alyssa, back near the exit door, flicked a gaze flicked past Kylie's shoulder. The hard woman's eyes widened.

Mac tensed.

Just as Kylie finally clued in to why Tibor had sent John and not Maksim to get Sam some boots, she turned her head to see the large Russian bodyguard aiming a large handgun which he'd obviously found somewhere in the hallway, at Ogano. With Samantha in between.

Galette screamed.

And Kylie made one of the most foolhardy moves of her life.

# 26

WITH NO CONSCIOUS THOUGHT but a lightning prayer, Kylie spun and jumped directly in front of Maksim. "Don't shoot!" she said.

The big man's outstretched gun leapt ceiling-ward, his taut breath exploding in a Russian curse. Kylie heard Ogano scream something in Japanese and Tibor shouted, "*Nyet!*"

Everything froze. Galette tried to squeak out a translation, but Sato Sr. Cut her off.

"My son says now we take women, shoot all you. This not be." He spoke harshly in Japanese to his son and Kylie, eyes still fixed on Maksim's broad face, heard Ogano whining like a frustrated dog. "We take just our women."

Then, with Kylie's legs threatening to collapse under her, her heart started beating again. Her hands, she realized, were up in rigid talons on either side of her as if she could have caught any bullets Maksim shot. Pain shot through them as they released. But her chest jumped and sucked in air. Her head rushed with heat.

"Kylie!" commanded Hachiuma Sato's voice behind her.

Almost without volition, she turned and took in the scene. Tibor was on his knees now, face rigid. Ogano was white-faced with anger. He held his gun pressed hard into Tibor's temple. Sam and Galette were huddled together beside them. John was at the fireplace with a pair of boots in his hands and his jaw hanging down. Smythe was back in his original corner trying to look invisible. Alyssa and Mac—*Mac!*—stood coolly by the main door leading out.

"Kylie!" repeated Sato Sr. from the center of the room. "Come!"

Feeling Maksim and his large pistol behind her, the sparking electricity of Ogano directly ahead, Kylie took one involuntary step. Another.

"Don't I get my goodbye?" Mac said suddenly.

Kylie stopped, her heart instantly in her throat. Sato Sr. frowned and turn his head.

"You said I could say goodbye as a gift for saving your life," Mac said casually. "Are you a man of your word?"

Ogano said something guttural. Sato Sr. didn't respond. Holding Mac's gaze, he finally nodded and stepped to one side. "Mac," Alyssa said, like Mac was still hers.

But he wasn't. As he found Kylie's eyes and walked towards her, Kylie felt her heart speed at his approach. If Mac was anyone's ever again, she knew, he had to be Kylie's.

Then he reached her and his hands rose up to lightly grip her upper arms. Even with all the adrenaline that had been rushing through her body a moment ago, the simple touch still made her tingle. But her mouth was dry, her face hot. She couldn't speak.

"You're incredible," he whispered.

Her tongue was stuck. All she could do was nod.

In this improbable situation, he drew her in towards himself and she had not even the strength to raise her hands as feebly as she had that night in the Creekside. She merely watched, amazed, as he lips descended to hers. When they touched, parched but gentle, her eyes closed automatically and she felt in another world as the lips slid to the side along her cheek and came to rest beside her ear.

"I'm just looking for an opening," Mac whispered. "When you're near the door. We have to have an exit. Play along with Sato but try to stay on the outside."

"The hallway. There's a back way out," she whispered.

He was already pulling back and she couldn't know if he'd hear her. Her eyes shot wide and met his—male, calm, apparently amused, as if the goodbye were nothing more than an exercise of his prerogative.

"Okay," he said to Sato Sr. "She's all yours."

A cell phone beeped. The sound came from Mac. Mac held up his hand. "Just a minute."

As casually as if they were in a quiet party, Macaulay tugged his cell phone out of ski jacket pocket, flipped it open and held it up to his ear. Listened. "Really," he said after a second. "Yes, that's right. See you soon."

He snapped it closed and shoved it back into his jacket pocket. "You should probably know," he said to Sato Sr., "that the police are on their way here. The road out is blocked off. They finally got their warrants to search this place. And all this?" Mac waved his hand at Ogano with his gun still pressed to Tibor's head, Maksim with his own pistol now aimed at Ogano again, Slava lying possibly dead on the floor between them. "This won't look good."

There was a long pause. Kylie thought she could hear the hammering of all ten hearts in the room.

Tibor, forcing himself to speak slowly, said, "There is a way out. If we move fast. This deal is not broken. It was just a misunderstanding, yes? There is a way. Galette, translate."

Looking relieved to be ordered to do something, Galette babbled it out in what sounded like seamless Japanese.

Ogano's eyes snapped back towards his father, careful not to take his gun from Tibor's temple. He said something fast in Japanese. Sato Sr. answered.

"He *lie!*" Ogano spat, gesturing with his chin towards Mac.

Mac shrugged. "Suit yourself."

Father and son spoke again, then Ogano barked. "Boot!"

It took John, by the fireplace, a moment to realize this was directed at him. When he did, he jumped forward, hurrying to Samantha and kneeling down to help her slide her bare feet into them. Sam's gaze shot to Kylie's and were filled with such hopeless fear that Kylie wanted to run to her, put her body between Ogano and her this time. Whatever it took.

Kylie didn't move, though, trusting Mac. Hoping.

The boots were on. John stood. Ogano snarled at him. "Coat."

John looked about helplessly. The only winter jackets in sight were those being worn by the Mac, the Satos, Tibor, and Galette.

"Coat!" Ogano shouted.

John grabbed Galette's sleeve and tugged. She tugged back, then seem to realize this meant she wouldn't have to leave with the others. She quickly unzipped her jacket completely and shrugged it off. Handed it to Samantha, who tugged it on over her skimpy dress.

Ogano grunted and raised Tibor to standing. Sato Sr. said

something in Japanese and Ogano grunted again, but pulled the gun back from Tibor's head. The thin Russian looked down at the toad-like Ogano, shook back his hair so the red mark from the gun barrel on his temple shone angrily, then motioned to Maksim to lower his gun too.

"It's time to go," Tibor said nodded them all towards the main exit door.

Maksim lowered his gun and stepped towards Ogano and Samantha, Tibor, and the turning figure of Sato Sr.

"John?" said Macaulay. "You heard them."

Kylie felt, as much as saw, Mac lunge for her.

~~~~

When they were kids, John had always been the one running to keep up to Mac. His big brother was always taller, faster, stronger, braver. John was the tag-along, the pest, almost three years younger and willing to do anything to be included in Mac's schemes.

So, even though John had followed Mac through university with marks every bit as good, carved out a career in corporate law that had him shooting to be one of the youngest partners in one of the town's preeminent firms, stolen Mac's wife away from him, there was still a programmed response buried deep inside him that Mac's calm words triggered.

It was a clear command to plunge after his big brother in another harebrained adventure.

And, common sense be damned, John did exactly that.

~~~~

As Mac grabbed Kylie and rushed her across the room with him, he saw his brother coming through in the clutch. John grabbed Samantha from Ogano's arm and dragged her backwards in the direction Mac was running. The Satos, even criminal masterminds that they were, staggered around in surprise. Tibor shouted something in Russian. Maksim whirled around.

But Mac was at the hallway door. He shoved Kylie through it. Then things fell apart.

John tripped. Mac turned to grab him and saw that he'd *been* tripped by a large beefy arm sweeping the floor in wash of blood. Slava! Not dead. Mac's hand swung wide.

Mac staggered and John fell, tugging with him. Kylie screamed, "Sam!" from behind and leaped back past Mac into the great room. A sudden pile driver from Maksim hit Mac in the chest and drove him back to the wall.

Before a second blow could come to knock out his lights, though, he saw the huge Russian turn, grab both Samantha and Kylie, and literally throw both sisters towards the Satos and Tibor.

Mac felt his breath coming in wheezes as he pushed off the wall. He could hardly see. The room was tilting crazily on him. Then a figure registered—Ogano Sato, screaming something incomprehensible and raising his gun, pointing it at Mac.

With a last rush of survival instinct, Mac threw himself sideways and backwards, hitting the hallway opening and tumbling through it. He slammed the door shut with his foot, then managed to lunge up to it and threw the lock.

A bullet cracked through it. Something whumped against it. Something big enough to shake the hinges.

Gulping air, brain whirring, Mac leapt to his feet, pounded

his feet on the floor and hit the wall, then shouted, "Yeah! They're right in there. Along with the kidnaped girls! Hurry!"

He made more noise but heard over it the frantic scramble on the other side of the door in the great room. Brain afire, he got set to fling open the door and run after them, but something even stronger, a calculating part of his brain that had always been there in the heat of trial to weigh the odds and sort through a hundred options a second, made him stop. Because only he knew that the police weren't here. The phone call had been from Joey, asking when he was going to get his suit back.

Taking a huge rasping breath, Mac turned and began running down the hallway to find the back exit Kylie had whispered about.

# 27

$M$*AC!* Kylie's heart cried as Maksim dragged her down the narrow staircase after the fleeing assortment of criminals and kidnap victims.

She looked wildly around as they spilled out the bottom and straight out the outer door of the lodge. She heard no police sirens, no bullhorn shouts to stop.

Yet in Maksim's iron grip, there was no way she could flee or signal even if she'd seen them.

Ahead of her, Samantha was being hurried along by Ogano with less than a lover's gentleness. Ahead of them was Sato Sr., talking quickly with Tibor, who was gesturing ahead of him and up the tallest of the resort mountains, the one Mac had named Schlatter.

Clutched by Tibor's right hand was the skinny, sweater-clad arm of Alyssa Rush. Tibor had grabbed her as they'd all rushed out, confirming Mac's earlier guess that Alyssa and John weren't exactly secure in their marriage.

Left behind had been Galette, Jerome Smythe, and John, presumably because they were not wanted, or maybe because they figured they could talk their way out of whatever the police tried to pin on them.

Now, as Kylie stumbled and almost stepped out of her felt boot-slippers that Slava had stuck on her last night, she saw where her running group was going.

A Snow Cat, a big yellow passenger truck on tank treads designed for climbing ski slopes. The hills just outside of Kylie's home back in Madison had one, though the size of the hills and duration of season hardly warranted it. All she knew was they roared loudly and went uphill really fast.

Tibor reached the vehicle and jumped up, yanking open the double doors that swung wide to open up the entire back and yelling loudly to two men standing on the far side of it. One of them jumped up and ran to the front door of the Cat. He was inside and revving the engine by the time the Ogano had dragged Samantha and Maksim had dragged Kylie, up to the back door. Both men loaded in their women like so much luggage and climbed in behind them.

They pulled the doors shut and the schoolbus-stye bench seats lurched forward. With a roar of the engine, the Cat took off in a sharp turn and headed up the slope almost parallel to the chairlift.

"Kylie?" Samantha sniffed, craning her neck to look around Ogano at her sister. Kylie, hemmed in by Maksim's bulk, could see Sam's eyes were red and frightened. Pleading for reassurance.

But what could Kylie do? She'd put so much trust in Mac and now he was gone, maybe shot? Lying bleeding somewhere?

She made herself shut down that train of thought. It wasn't helping.

Still, what could Kylie do against all these men? She didn't even know where they were taking them. Away from the resort, obviously. Maybe down some trail over the mountain that bypassed the police roadblock. Maybe they'd get stuck or tip over and Kylie and Sam could...

What?

As they clanked and roared higher, Kylie considered what Samantha was wearing, what she herself was wearing on her feet. If they escaped in some snowy ravine somewhere, they would never make it out. If she and Sam were to escape, it had to be soon.

She took a breath of sharp, cold air and looked around. She and Sam were hemmed in on the sides, but in front or behind?

Behind them were the doors. Locked.

Directly in front of Kylie sat Hachiuma Sato, the grey bristles of his neck sticking up over the collar of his ski jacket, his hands chopping the air vigorously. To his left, nodding calmly, sat Tibor. The two men were obviously using the roar of the Snow Cat to cover ongoing negotiations.

Could she use that?

Across the mini-aisle to Tibor's left, her arms wrapped around herself and shivering, was the only one not wearing a ski jacket— Alyssa Rush. Her top was beautiful, white angora that hugged her rail-thin body and set off her hair, shiny brown like Kylie's own. Her fine features, with their chattering teeth, just bordered on sharp, like Kylie's. In many ways she and Kylie could have twins. It probably explained Mac's instant attraction to her. Maybe he'd never given up loving Alyssa?

Strangely the thought didn't make Kylie feel sorry for herself; it released a sudden gush of sympathy for the woman. Alyssa was yesterday's model. By her own choosing, perhaps, because she'd been too caught up in herself to see what had been right in front of her the whole time.

"Alyssa!" Kylie called over the roar of the Cat.

There was no response beyond Maksim's glare and she called again. Alyssa finally turned her shivering form and looked at her. Not entirely sure why she was doing it, Kylie shrugged out of her ski jacket and threw it forward to Alyssa. The woman caught it, looked down at it, then looked back up at Kylie, confused.

"Put it on!" Kylie called, fighting off her own urge to wrap her arms around herself and start shivering.

After a beat, Alyssa nodded, then reached quickly down and lifted up her own sweater, pulling it over her head to reveal a silky white top underneath. She tossed the sweater to Kylie, bouncing it off Tibor's head in flight, and had pulled on Kylie's jacket by the time Kylie caught it and figured out which end was up.

The Snow Cat lurched and jolted over some sharp dip the driver hadn't managed to avoid and Tibor growled at him.

Then Kylie had on Alyssa's sweater. She wrapped her arms around herself, and began rubbing and shivering. Alyssa was not even looking at her.

Hey, good start, Kylie thought to herself. Want to give your snow slippers away now too?

~~~~

Mac saw the Snow Cat disappear behind a ridge up the mountain as he ran towards the Schlatter chairlift. His left arm carried his borrowed snowboard. His right hand swung his cell phone back and forth, trying to keep a good signal to 9-1-1.

"Up...the mountain," he panted into the phone. "I *told* you.

Two guns. Two hostages."

"Sir," the 9-1-1 female was saying calmly over the crackle, "you need to tell me your full name and location."

"Damn it!" Mac shouted into the cell as he reached the lift area and threw down the snowboard. "Just put me through to the RCMP. Sergeant Dickson. Commander Dickson. Whatever the hell he's called."

"What dctachment, Sir?"

"Lion's Bay. North Vancouver. I don't know. He's supposed to be on his way up here. Mobile unit, maybe."

"I don't have a way to connect you there, Sir."

"Well do *some*thing!"

"Yes, Sir. I'll transfer you."

The line crackled out.

"Aghh!" Mac shouted and wanted to throw the phone back the way he'd come. Instead he jammed it into his pocket and shoved his left boot into the snowboard binding, did it up, and pushed himself rapidly up into the instructor's line.

"Hey, Mac," said the liftie as he slid up. "You okay?"

"Just let me on," Mac snapped. "No one with me."

"Whoah," the eighteen-year-old said. "Sure, man."

He held back the others and Mac caught the next chair. As he swung past the first pylon, he heard a roaring sound below and looked back to the right to see a snowmobile heading up the mountain the way the Snow Cat had gone. Its helmeted driver swerved wildly to avoid a skier descending and something in the panicky move and recovery twigged Mac's recognition.

That ski jacket! The pants! It was John! Had to be! What was he thinking?

Mac smashed a hand against the side of the chair, willing it to go faster. He had to reach Kylie now. Forget about catching Tibor and the Yakuza as long as he saved her and her sister. Despite his nickname "Gunner", Mac knew he could never have been a prosecutor. He was a rescuer, born with shining armor on. What could you do?

But if the police didn't get up here soon to help him out...

He gritted his teeth and swung his head around to look out towards the road coming in to Milaya Ridge.

He *had* told 9-1-1 about the helicopter pad on the east shoulder of Schlatter, hadn't he?

$$\sim\sim\sim\sim$$

Kylie felt as much as saw or heard the thudding blades of a helicopter landing. But it didn't register at first.

A helicopter on a ski hill?

Then she recalled seeing it whirring around her first day here. She'd asked Bo about it back when she still thought he was just a helpful liftie. He'd said it was for tourist sightseeing.

And now?

Kylie stopped rubbing her arms long enough to half stand in her feet, trying to see past Tibor and Hachiuma. Maksim pulled her back down, but not roughly. He too seemed puzzled by the direction the Snow Cat was taking, down a side trail from the main ski track onto the shoulder of the mountain. Here the resort designers had carved out or found a natural small bowl in the hillside and run the track into its base, where they'd poured concrete for a helipad. A mini-café sat up on the edge of the bowl where heli-sightseers could wait for their flight or just take a break and watch the machine take off and land.

The Cat was roaring down the track towards the scraped helipad where the helicopter had landed and was slowing its blades.

"This?" Kylie heard Hachiuma ask Tibor and the Russian nodded.

As the Cat came to a lurching halt, Hachiuma turned in his seat to speak to his son. Kylie saw the younger Sato's face drain of all color. He pulled out his gun again and began shouting in Japanese, shaking his head violently.

Sam started wailing. Tibor nodded to Maksim to open the rear doors. Maksim did, dragging Kylie out behind him as he flung them open. From inside the Cat came sounds of Ogano Sato getting hysterical. He obviously didn't like to fly. How, Kylie wondered, had they ever managed to get him over here in the first place?

That became evident a second later as the sounds suddenly ceased and Sato Sr. emerged. The Japanese Yakuza boss looked around, sniffed the air, then turned back to the open rear doors. He gestured imperiously and the Cat driver came running around from the front to help Tibor carry out Ogano. He was unconscious, whether by karate chop or some quick anesthetic, Kylie couldn't tell.

Samantha cowered behind, trying to catch Kylie's eye as if to get confirmation she should make a break for it.

But before Kylie could confirm that the café up on the side of the bowl looked deserted, the area completely cleared on non-Milaya staff, Tibor had turned with Ogano's gun and ordered Sam and Alyssa out.

They came, Sam cowering, Alyssa looking coldly from Tibor to the Japanese and back.

"Maksim," Tibor ordered, "get young Sato-san into the helicopter. The rest of us will follow." He waved his gun at Kylie to emphasize the point.

But Kylie had been slowly inching away from Maksim so that she now stood almost five feet from the rest of them. If she ran now, dodging back and forth, could she make it up the side of the bowl without being shot? Reach the other side and the trees there? Samantha would be left, but Kylie could call the cops, tell them where she was. Kylie had to do *some*thing.

Her heart pounding, she hesitated just long enough to catch Tibor's attention, when a high-pitched roaring tore everyone's gaze left. Blasting down the same path the Snow Cat had followed, a cloud of snow ripping up behind it, came a blood-red Skidoo.

It aimed right for the center of the crowd near the helicopter, swerving to avoid the prostrate body of Ogano Sato as the others scattered, then skidded to a stop beside Kylie and ordered her to "Jump on!" The Skidoo operator's visor was half-covered in snow and fog and he swiped at it wildly to clear it even as she jumped on behind him, wrapped her arms around his torso, and he blasted them out of there.

The sound of a gunshot made her want to turn back. Shouting. Tibor. Kylie buried her face into the jacket of her driver and just held on.

The driver roared them up the side of the bowl towards the café, keeping the helicopter between them and Tibor's group, then swerved right at the last moment to jump high over the lip, sending Kylie's heart into her throat.

They landed with a whump, snapping Kylie's head forward painfully, and the driver skidded them to a halt. He jumped off, helping her off, then yanked off his helmet. "Allie, are you—?"

Kylie pushed back her hair and reflected John Rush's stupefied expression. Then it clicked. The sweater. She was wearing Alyssa's sweater. Also her jeans, her same brown hair.

John hadn't been trying to save Kylie at all.

But Tibor! Wouldn't he be sending Maksim after her? Wasn't she needed to clinch his deal with Hachiuma Sato?

Kylie whirled and ran towards the café, hoping to hide there or call for help, when she heard two things simultaneously. From the distance, floating up the hill like weird bagpipe music, came the sound of police sirens. Closer in Tibor shouted, "Now! Now! Get everyone get in!"

Throwing herself flat to the snow near the edge, Kylie saw Maksim carry Ogano Sato under the helicopter blades and shrug him into the craft. Then Tibor, his eyes jumping now and then to the lip of the bowl where John had roared Kylie out, waved in the rest of the crew with Ogano's gun. He jumped in after them as the engine started whining and the long helicopter blades began to rotate.

Alyssa, Hachiuma Sato, Samantha, Tibor himself. With Maksim, Ogano, and the pilot, that made seven people aboard. Eight if you counted the oversized Maksim as two. The helicopter didn't look big enough. And wasn't the air supposed to be thinner up here? Just how much could that little craft lift?

Indeed, as its blades reached liftoff speed, the craft rocked back and forth hesitantly. The snow on the concrete landing pad and all the ground snow around the bowl billowed around it in a white cloud. The helicopter inched off the ground.

Kylie's peripheral vision saw John running towards her. He dove down beside her on the snow. "Damn it," he said in way that made Kylie think of Mac. Her heart clenched. She shook it off.

Her sister, her baby sister whom she'd tracked all the way here and even held in her arms last night, was being taken away.

"We've got to stop them," Kylie said, rising.

"It's too late," John said.

Kylie wasn't listening. She was already up and running down the slope towards the crazy, oversized metal bird that rocked before her in a cloud of blowing snow, trying to find its direction.

Just when she thought she was going to be able to reach it and grab onto one of its skids, the bird found its balance, turned and began sloughing back in the direction away from her, towards the way the Snow Cat had come. They must be headed over the mountain's shoulder, out some back valley where Samantha would vanish forever. Kylie yelled after it in panic and seemed to shake it. It dipped a bit towards the lip of the bowl, started to rise over it...

And a man-sized purple gnat suddenly flew from the lip of the bowl to attach itself to the helicopter's left skid.

The helicopter bucked sideways and sloughed back into the bowl towards Kylie, making her stumble back and fall onto her behind, the ground snow whipping up around her.

But through it all Kylie's face shone with wonder.

*Mac. It was Mac.*

Macaulay Rush , had rocketed up the outside of the bowl as the helicopter cleared it and done a go-for-broke jump to grab the helicopter skid then wrap his arms around it. Now he hung on for dear life with his snowboard swinging wildly under him.

The helicopter slid down towards Kylie again, then turned around and rocked the other way, blowing hurricane winds and cutting ice at Kylie as the pilot fighting to center it in the bowl. It was only fifteen or twenty feet off the ground now, seemingly unable to rise further. Mac had stopped them!

Kylie jumped to her feet, hair blowing about wildly, and wondered if she could grab onto Mac's wildly swinging snowboard, pull him down with her weight. Only...that would just pull the helicopter down on top of both of them.

The side door of the chopper opened and as it swung around her way, she saw Maksim there, holding it open, while Tibor held onto the side with one hand, and aimed Ogano's big gun with the other.

Aimed it at Mac.

"No!" Kylie screamed, and ran directly below Mac, reaching for his snowboard, still too high above her.

Tibor swung the barrel of the pistol down towards Kylie.

# 28

MAC'S CHEST, still raw from the slam Maksim had given it earlier, felt like it was ripping in two. The helicopter kept swinging, a wild flying whale he was trying to bring back to earth.

Then Kylie screamed below him, he looked down and saw her, looked back up and saw Tibor aiming his gun at her, and felt his life about to end. All of this for nothing. He'd just made it worse.

But Maksim seemed to stumble against Tibor suddenly, knocking the gun from his hand.

"*Khokhol!*" Tibor screeched at Maksim over the clatter of the blades.

"I have a sister!" Maksim shouted back.

The helicopter tilted drunkenly down on Mac's side and Tibor tumbled out, only to be caught by Maksim. As the big man started to haul him in, there was a sudden loud crack and the metal to the right of Maksim's head splintered off.

Mac looked down to see Kylie with Tibor's dropped gun raised up in a two-handed grip, aiming at the Tibor, Maksim, whomever she could get a bead on as the helicopter swung in the air.

The helicopter paused then sloughed wildly the other direction, throwing Maksim, still holding Tibor, back inside.

"Shoot at the rear!" Mac shouted down to Kylie. "The fuel tanks!"

But he saw her face freeze in horror. Maybe that she'd shot at all, or just that it had been so close to hitting someone. As the helicopter swung around again, though, he saw her set her jaw and raise the gun again.

~~~~

Inside the rolling aircraft, the partner sighed at Tibor's wildly emotional dramatics and decided enough was enough.

She stood carefully in her snow-soaked Ugg boots, stepped over the cowering Michaelson bimbo and Ogano Sato's prostrate form laid out flat on the floor between the rows of seats, and leaned close to Hachiuma Sato's ear to speak over the roar and thudding chatter of the helicopter.

"*Hai!*" the Yakuza boss nodded and the partner pulled back.

Grabbing quickly to the back of Hachiuma's seat as the helicopter tilted sickly backwards and sideways, she turned to where Tibor and Maksim lay tumbled against the back passenger wall.

"Give me your gun!" she shouted at the oversized bodyguard.

Maksim blinked stupidly at her as he struggled to disentangle himself.

"*Da,*" she heard Tibor say.

Maksim fumbled his Uzzi out of his jacket and handed it to Alyssa.

"*Spatzibah!*" she thanked him mockingly and took it. She

turned it on Tibor and Maksim. "Even without our hanger on, we're too heavy!" she shouted. "Sato's agreed we ditch the girl and Maksim!"

Tibor hesitated, still helpless in his tumble, and Alyssa turned to Samantha with the gun. "You!" she ordered. "Out! Now!"

Samantha stared at her dumbly and Alyssa swung the gun to fire one stutter of shots out the open door to wake her up. The blond scrambled out of her seat just as the aircraft rolled towards the door side again and the girl almost tumbled out.

"Incompetent male drivers," Alyssa mumbled and pointed the submachine gun again at Samantha Michaelson. "Jump!"

"*Nyet*!" Maksim shouted and finally managed to extricate himself from Tibor. "I will drop her!"

~~~~

Down on the snow, Kylie moved the barrel of the pistol back and forth, trying to find something on the rear of the weaving helicopter that looked like a gas tank.

But the tail was moving too fast and snow kept blowing into her eyes so she could hardly see.

The door of helicopter! Kylie swung her sights back towards it and tightened her finger on the trigger. The wind from the propeller blades made her arms weave back and forth. But even with Mac swinging around up there, even with Samantha in the chopper itself, if she had one clear shot, she'd—

There! Two legs, a body, above it Maksim's bulk leaning out. Aim...

Kylie gasped and pulled back her arms as she saw the legs were bare above the boots. Sam's legs. They were extending out the rocking door, further, then further still, and Kylie saw she was being lowered as far down as possible by Maksim. He was going to drop her! But she was still a good twenty feet above Kylie, above the hard pavement.

As the helicopter bucked up then down for a moment, Maksim let her go.

Kylie ran under her and Sam's body hit her in a whump that drove her to the concrete. Her head hit and everything went black.

~~~~

Mac's first clue that Samantha was coming out was when the helicopter dipped to the right and smashed her arm and Maksim's knobby hand against his shoulder blades.

Mac whipped his head around to see just as Samantha dropped down onto Kylie, hitting Kylie's chest feet first and snapping her down. Though he couldn't hear the crack of her head, he felt it like a knife through his own.

With a surge of rage, he tried to swing the helicopter around. But just then a second whump in his back told him someone else had come out. Someone bigger.

He looked back to find Maksim's hairy face grinning down at him from where the big Russian held onto the lip of the door. "Good luck," he said.

The helicopter was already rising since Samantha's weight was gone. Now, as Maksim let go, the machine leapt upwards at an angle, screaming over the edge of the bowl with Mac scrambling to hold onto the round metal skid for dear life. But he was slipping. He was nearly deaf. His arms and chest, beaten by Maksim and now ripped back and forth in this craziness, were senseless, the strength in them gone.

They shot over the edge of the shoulder onto the backside of Schlatter, the supposed bear sanctuary that Tibor wanted to destroy and take over.

And, thought Mac in instant admiration as he was whipped over it, he could see why. Beautiful drops. Serious powder. Major vertical.

Dropping from here would be like riding over a hundred foot cliff. It was doable, though. If you were insane. And if you could land it right...*there.*

He let go.

# 29

THE HOSPITAL CORRIDOR WHERE KYLIE PACED hummed with a bad florescent light ballast. Nurses scurried by silently with trays and clipboards, not looking at her. As if she were somehow to blame for the condition of the man in Room 16.

Which she was, of course. She'd dragged him into her crazy search for Samantha. And somehow, Kylie felt, his involvement had triggered Ogano Sato's desire to buy Sam. It had certainly triggered Hachiuma Sato's desire to buy Kylie.

Which had led to the mountaintop, which had led to the helicopter, to Macaulay having to prove himself, to him almost dying.

The female doctor who'd put Mac's shattered leg and ribs back together came out of his room with a thoughtful look. She saw Kylie staring at her.

"You're family?"

Kylie shook her head. Mac's family lived on the other side of the country. His only family out here, John, had already been in then out again. He and Jerome were apparently up to their ears between answering police questions and trying to prepare for the application Mac had brought to turn Milaya Ridge over to its early investors. The resort itself was temporarily shut down and therefore hemorrhaging money.

"I'm a friend," she said.

The doctor nodded. "He's going to need those. Go on in."

Kylie bit her lip and did.

The room was brightly lit, with the horizontal blinds fully

raised to let in the sun and the sight of the mountains in the distance. Sun glinted off the snow up there.

The figure in the bed, Macaulay Rush, lay flat back in his bed, staring out at the sight. His entire left side looked immobilized in some kind of metal gear the doctor had thoughtfully covered with a sheet. He didn't turn to look at Kylie when she walked in.

"The doctor says that was some kind of record jump you did," Kylie said. "She was amazed you didn't compress or rupture your entire spine."

"People have been cliff jumping 1500 feet since '96. 3000 feet off Kjerag in Norway a few years back. I just landed wrong."

The coldness of his voice sent a shiver through her. "Sam's okay. She and the other girls are on a treatment program for methamphetamine addiction."

That made him close his eyes and turn his head slightly. "It'll be hard for her."

"My own head crack wasn't serious." She reached up and touched the back of her head. It was still tender. "Mostly lack of food that made me go into shock."

"I heard."

"And they arrested just about everyone—all the Yakuza, Bo, Slava, and Maksim. I put in a good word for Maksim when Samantha explained what he did. The others—Alyssa, Tibor, and the Satos—they got when they landed on the stolen barge just off the coast. Seems someone alerted the police that they might be going there. The coast guard boarded it an hour before and were waiting when the helicopter set down."

Mac's face cracked half a smile. "I just figured Tibor would still be using Daddy's stuff as a backup plan. He'd run his human cargo out on the barge to meet an ocean-going ship. Easier than airports."

"Which meant you and John never had to rescue us. We could have just landed there and been safe."

The smile dropped and Mac looked away. "John didn't know. I couldn't be sure."

"Mac," Kylie pleaded, her heart squeezing so painfully at the way he shut her out that she felt *she* had the broken ribs. "I'm so sorry I pulled you into this. I'm sorry I let myself get caught. Sorry I couldn't get away earlier somehow. I'm...sorry."

He looked back at her surprised. "It's not your fault."

"Then what is it? What did I do? Why won't you talk to me? Can't you see I love you?"

That seemed to rock him, and for just a moment his face opened up to her in a kind of wonder laced with pain. Then it slammed shut again.

"That's not a good plan," he said.

"Yeah, well I'm funny that way," Kylie said, her face growing hot. "I don't tend to plan this sort of thing."

"You should. You're too impulsive."

"Look who's talking."

His eyes narrowed and mouth tightened. He shook his head and turned away. "I'm really tired now. Thanks for coming by."

"I'm so glad I did," she said. She wanted to grab him, shake him. What was wrong with him?

But when he said nothing more, Kylie finally turned and walked out of the room, closing the door behind her just a touch too firmly. She stood outside it with her own jaw clenched and her clenched fists shaking, trying to sort out the wild crash of emotions inside.

She'd just told him that she loved him. Did he think she casually tossed that out to every man she met? Or did he, despite his words, blame her for ending up in this hospital with no job and the chance he'd maybe never walk normally again? *Was* that her fault? Was she just being stupid hanging on here, looking for something in him that he'd never truly felt?

"He is a difficult man," said a gravelly Russian voice behind her.

She turned to see Leonid Balakirev, his thick body and pouchy eyes looking even heavier in the corridor light. His trench coat and suit reeked of cigarettes. His eyes and skin sagged with a yellow pallor. His right hand clutched a bouquet of spring flowers. He shrugged when he saw her look there.

"A difficult man but a good friend," he said.

"I told him I loved him," Kylie blurted.

"He did not take this well."

Kylie shook her head. She had to bite her tongue to stop the sudden swell of tears.

"You know why."

She shook her head again.

The older Russian looked her over then nodded his head to the side. "Come and sit down. Let us talk together."

She nodded and sat in one of the bench of plastic chairs in the hallway. Balakirev settled his bulk into the one beside her.

"Was Mac a good lawyer?" she asked before he could speak.

"Yes. He was. He is. One of the best. He seems so easygoing, yes? But he was known as being stubborn. Principled. He never gave up a fight."

"Until Melanie Carson. Then he gave up on everything."

Balakirev sagged his head and rubbed his nose. His meaty hands patted at his pockets, searching for cigarettes apparently, because once they found a package in his trench pocket, he stared at them and shoved them back into his pocket, relieved.

"We all have...weak spots," Balakirev sighed. "Macaulay was hit in his weak spot too many times too quickly. He staggered a bit."

"Quit his job. Became a snow bum."

"Staggered a lot, maybe." As if his own willpower cut out, the Russian fumbled back into his trench pocket, pulled out his cigarette package and removed one, sticking it between his lips, unlit. He closed his eyes and leaned back his head against the wall. "You know what he told me the other day in my office?"

"What?"

"That he had finally found someone who made him want to try again. She was someone strong, good. She scared him a little, though, because she was as pigheaded as he used to be. He worried about the danger this put her in. I had already warned him about this."

Kylie said nothing.

"Ten minutes later, someone was trying to run his woman down with a truck. The next day they kidnaped her and tried to take her away from him." Leonid opened her eyes and turned his head to look at her. "He has had too many people leave him."

Kylie stared down at her shoes. Leonid sat up and pushed his bulk out of the chair. He picked up his bouquet and walked to the door of Mac's hospital room.

"Wait," Kylie said. "What should I do?"

"If you love him?" Leonid asked.

"Yes."

He pulled the unlit cigarette from his lips and shoved it into his trench pocket. "Don't leave."

~~~~

To Mac's amazement and discomfiture, Kylie showed up in his hospital room the next day. And the next. And the day after that.

When he finally transferred into the rehab wing to begin relearning to walk, she came twice a day, staying for his rehab session, then coming again at dinnertime with something that inevitably smelled better than the hospital cuisine.

Then, one week into rehab, she came only after dinner and Mac was amazed at how short he became with everyone, and how elated he was when she arrived. Two days later she didn't show up at all and Mac was so angry he called up his secretary and had her ship the entire Milaya Ridge file to the hospital so he could plunge back into it.

When Kylie showed up the day after that, Mac's heart leapt to see her walking in. But he quickly clenched it down and watched her warily. She moved his files and document boxes to the end of the bed and unpacked her usual dinnertime spread as if she'd never been away.

"Where were you?" he said.

She raised her eyebrows at him. By unspoken covenant, they hadn't talked about her ongoing presence in his life. Nor about what had happened, other than Kylie giving him brief updates on Samantha's progress. He and Kylie hadn't kissed. They hadn't touched except where necessary, though even these contacts had been starting to drive Mac wild. Each day, in fact, he'd found himself weaving increasingly intricate fantasies that usually involved Kylie in substantially fewer clothes than she usually wore to visit him.

Then this. She'd just vanished. How could he tell her now how close he'd been to finally dropping the front and admitting he needed her? More than ever needed Alyssa, in fact, because when he'd married her he'd been cocky and untried in life. Now he'd run through the fire of failure and was finally coming out the other end. Wiser. Knowing his limits. Knowing also that it was right to push them for a good cause and accept the blows that came with it.

Even the blow of losing Kylie, but he so hoped that—

"My sabbatical from Nieman Marcus ran out," she said. "I have to go back to work."

Mac's heart plunged like his drop from the helicopter. Nothing below. Falling. *Falling.* "So you're leaving."

"No. My boss had a friend up here in Holt Renfrew who was looking for a store manager. She encouraged me to interview for the position. I did that last week. I had to fly to their head office on Wednesday to meet everyone else. Today I met the buyers who will be working for me."

"You're...staying."

Kylie stopped what she was doing and met his eyes with her own. "For as long as you'll have me."

And inside he landed his drop so cleanly that he swooshed through the untouched powder like a god. A laugh escaped from his mouth and he reached out for her hands. She solemnly gave them, warm and dry, but her face stayed serious. Waiting.

"Kylie Michaelson," he said. "I will have you for as long as you'll stay."

"Officially?" Her eyes were sparkling wet. "With no more secrets? No more holding back?"

"You pick the date."

"Oh, Mac." Like she'd been waiting for her own landing, Kylie leaned forward, gently gathering his hands and forearms into hers and squeezing them like she truly would never let him go.

Then she drew back. "I already know who'll be a maid of honor. Alongside Sam, of course."

"Who?"

"Someone Leonid introduced me too. A charming young woman you've apparently been putting through technical school for the last few years. Did you know she graduates in two months? Very proud of herself. Very grateful to the lawyer who never quit on her."

"Melanie Carson."

She nodded happily. "Any other secrets I should know about?"

"Just one," Mac said, pulling her closer so their lips were inches apart. "The delicacy of my physical condition right now? It's been grossly overstated."

"Oh really?" she breathed. "Prove it."

And very carefully, but with great resolve, he did exactly that.

# About the Author

Terri Darling lives with her family in the Pacific Northwest, where she writes sensual, suspenseful, and sweet romance. You can find more about her and her work at www.terridarling.com.

# Want more?

Read on for a sample from her romantic suspense *Last One to Hide*

An urgent plea for protection brings Richard Mackenzie home from Afghanistan on special leave. But when his mission to protect his brother and brother's family goes horribly wrong, he finds himself on the run with his 6-year-old niece and more questions than answers. And the one person who may be able to help him, a sister-in-law he's never met, poses a whole other kind of danger.

# LAST ONE TO HIDE
## Terri Darling

# 1

Bethesda, Maryland
late morning
Sunday

THE PHONE.

When it jingled out through the heat of the backyard gardens, Richard Mackenzie's head snapped up. If that was his brother's mysterious "Deep Throat" contact, he was twelve minutes past his scheduled call time. Richard had already let his brother's family stand down from reception mode and resume their normal lives on this hot Sunday afternoon.

"I got *you!* I got *you*, Daddy!"

"Oh yeah? Well take *that*, you little squirt gun monster!'"

Richard's brother, Tom Mackenzie, a handsome, twenty-eight-year-old government lawyer, chased his whirling-dervish of a daughter, Janine, in and out of the rhododendron bushes that lined the back of their property...just inside the detection wire Richard had strung up around the whole perimeter.

Richard was helping Tommy's wife, Marie-Ange, weed the

gardens closer to the house itself.

The phone rang again.

Tom still obviously hadn't heard it. But Tom's wife had. She knelt, frozen in place among the impatiens in the dirt of the long flowerbed directly behind the stone patio. Her back and curly blonde hair were to Richard, her heart-shaped face hidden from him, but he saw her tremble. And why not? Even though she knew nothing, Tom had made her his backup for these calls in case something happened to him.

Stupid. You give someone a job, you owe them the intel to do it properly.

On the third ring, Richard made a snap decision and leaned towards her from where he'd been bagging the weeds she pulled.

"You answer it," he whispered.

Visibly pale, Marie-Ange mopped her sweaty forehead with the back of a gardening glove, then tugged off the gloves, stood, and hurried inside the kitchen door of her and Tom's modern colonial.

Richard followed.

As she stopped at the butcher-block counters and reached for the wall phone, he held up a hand. "Wait."

Stepping beside her, he flicked on the modified Public-Safety Answering Point he'd insisted Tom let him set up this morning. The PSAP was a three-foot box of gray metal and plastic a friend of Richard's from U.S. Navy intelligence had "borrowed" from a mobile 9-1-1 unit. It stuck out like an eyesore in the homey kitchen. But the auto number and auto location controller (ANI/ALI) could still trace incoming calls in ten seconds if the call came from the greater DC area. And while its cell phone tracking was slower and dependent on which carrier brought the signal, it could still pinpoint the nearest cell tower coverage area within fifteen seconds, or the location within five meters if the user's phone sent a GPS signal.

The data flowed to the connected laptop computer. It also recorded calls and used a voice-stress analyzer to function as a crude lie detector.

Placing his hand on the PSAP's tapped-in second receiver, he caught his sister-in-law's gaze and said, "Go."

Marie-Ange picked up the phone receiver with Richard picking up his simultaneously. He stood almost shoulder-to-shoulder with her, noting distantly the slight gap in the front of her blouse, the smoothness of her cheek and neck, the smell of her floral perfume—violets, roses, something light. Once upon a time that would have stirred something in him. But that was before Afghanistan and the deadening of all such responses. Now the best he could do was say a silent congratulations to his younger brother. And swear to keep him alive to enjoy the life he'd built.

"Hello?" Marie-Ange said.

An intriguing contralto voice answered, "Hi, M.A."

There was a long beat of confusion on Marie-Ange's face and Richard frowned. According to Tom, his Deep Throat used some kind of voice distortion to protect his or her identity, hardly the show of trust Richard liked in someone Tommy was preparing to risk his life and his family's life for. So this wasn't Deep Throat?

Marie-Ange's eyes suddenly blinked wide. "Nina? Is that you?"

"Hey, Sis."

"Oh my God." Marie-Ange's face, pasty white split seconds ago, now flooded with color. "Neens! I didn't think you'd come!

When you didn't call me back. Nothing. And it's been..."

"Almost seven years, like you said."

"Just after Janine was born!" She was staring at Richard now with her eyes wide—forget-me-not blue, by God. Glistening with tears. His own face hardened and he thought that even if he'd still had the emotional freedom to lust, it wouldn't have been for this kind of woman. Marie-Ange was too sweet. She was like spun sugar that would crackle and melt when the going got tough. And in Richard's world, it always did.

He refocused on the phone call and the voice of this woman he'd never met, supposedly Marie-Ange's estranged sister.

The voice carried elevated stress levels. Richard didn't need the machine to tell him that. He could hear it as "Nina" began to talk, telling how she'd watched Marie-Ange's DVD. *Her what? How they'd have to talk about that.*

Something in the controlling tone of voice made Richard flash to a photo Tom had shown him once—Nina at some college function with her friends. She'd been taller than the other girls, thick brown hair and glasses, with a real presence that made her sexy. But it had all been ruined by her haughty expression. Richard had guessed, and Tom had confirmed, that she was an over-educated snob who wouldn't have been happy to know where Richard and Tom really hailed from.

Not that any of this would be hard to imitate on the phone by an impostor planning to draw Marie-Ange out of her protected zone. Was whoever Tom feared that devious? If it was the Russian mob, like Tom had hinted, they could be.

The ALI had pinpointed the caller in the 7400 block of Wisconsin Avenue, Bethesda, barely two miles away, a cellular call with GPS signal. Richard touched Marie-Ange's shoulder and pulled the receiver away from his ear, covering the mouthpiece and indicating she should do the same.

She did, staring at him in exasperation.

"Ask her where she's calling from."

Marie-Ange took her hand off the mouthpiece. "Where are you calling from, Nina?"

The voice gave a little snort. "Bethesda Station. I flew into the Reagan an hour ago and took the Red Line up here. *Such* a treat. I was going to just drop in on you, but figured I better give you some warning first in case your super-soldier shot me on sight. Is he there?"

"Yes, he's— Bethesda Station? You're right here?"

A cross-reference on the computer confirmed it. Which meant nothing if the whole point was to draw Marie-Ange out there, take her as a hostage. Almost like she'd read his mind, the voice on the phone asked for a pickup.

"Of course. Of course!" Marie-Ange gushed. "My God, I can't believe it! I'll be right out in just as quick as—"

Richard shook his head—*No*—and Marie-Ange frowned.

"Just a minute, Nina." She covered her receiver, with Richard copying the move. "Why not? It's ten minutes away by car. I'm wearing my beacon. This is my sister."

"Tell her to grab a taxi."

"But—"

"The phone line needs to be clear for Deep Throat's call. Clearing it in ten seconds." He held the phone to his ear with his shoulder, held up his ten fingers, and began silently counting them down.

Marie-Ange hurriedly spoke into the phone again. They had car trouble, she blurted, but lots of taxis came to the front of the Hyatt Hotel just across the street from the Station exit, Nina should take one, Marie-Ange would cover it when they got here, she was so thankful Nina had decided to come, and they'd catch up on everything just as soon as she arrived.

Then she slammed down the phone with a gasp of breath just as Richard's last finger fell and he too hung up.

Almost the same second, the phone rang again.

~~~~

Okay, Nina Tauredaux thought as she flipped her cell phone closed and pushed back her thick black hair. It was official. Marie-Ange was worse than ever and Nina was crazy for agreeing to come to her rescue.

The ribbed white roof of the Bethesda subway station converted the sounds of rushing people into garbled laughter, agreeing with her. But Marie-Ange's DVD-recorded plea hadn't really left her a choice, had it? It hadn't been the first time Nina's little bouncy, pretty, cheerleader, man-stealing sister had reached out with an apology and plea for Nina come back, but it was the first time Nina had tried to make it life and death.

And Marie-Ange had a child now, a six-year-old girl whom Nina had never even met. How could Nina not respond to help protect a little niece who, in another lifetime, could have been Nina's own?

Was it very sick that Nina was coming back as much to see that "might have been" as to help out her sister?

And if Tom Mackenzie just happened to do a double-take over how much Nina had improved herself these last seven years—she turned to catch a group of boys ogling her as they boarded the train, and she gave them a wicked smile and wave—well maybe that wouldn't be so bad either. He'd divorce Marie-Ange, sue for custody of little Janine, marry Nina, and move out west with her so they couldn't hear Marie-Ange howling in despair 24/7.

Or maybe they'd give Janine to Marie-Ange as a consolation prize. And Nina could give Tom electroshock treatments to wipe his memory. Then Tom and Nina could start over again, all fresh as dew and perfect as a rainbow.

Cue the Disney soundtrack.

Nina stopped in annoyance as her eyes started to leak. Damn pointy shoes! She knew she shouldn't have bought new shoes for this!

She sniffed, pushed back her unruly hair again, and grabbed the extended handle of her suitcase.

Okay, fine. So Nina was a bitch who was only coming back for all the wrong reasons. But Marie-Ange *did* ask her. So whatever happened, it was as much her fault as Nina's.

Dabbing lightly at her eyes to make sure her mascara hadn't run, he headed for the escalators to find a taxi.

~~~~

Richard saw Marie-Ange reach for the phone automatically, probably assuming it was an automatic call-back because the line hadn't disconnected properly.

Richard scooped his receiver up at the same time.

"Hello?" said Marie-Ange.

"Who is this?" came an electronically distorted voice. Deep Throat! Richard's earlier distraction was gone instantly. He saw the PSAP trying to get a fix on location. A DC lock! No. A router. At least one. The call had originated somewhere else. Whoever Deep Throat was, he or she obviously knew how to hack the carriers, or had the help of someone who did.

Marie-Ange, meanwhile, had almost dropped the phone in fright but Richard's free hand had steadied her wrist, feeling the sensation of her smooth skin, the delicate bones. Uncomfortably fragile. He noted that the shrieks and laughter had vanished outside. Tom and were probably on their way in.

"M-Marie-Ange here," she said.

Silence. Then, "I saw a flock of birds today."

Tight panic in Marie-Ange's eyes at the code words. Richard squeezed her wrist lightly. He knew Tom had given her the code answer. Richard just hoped she hadn't blanked in fear.

"Better...better birds than bombs," Marie-Ange said.

"Yes," the voice said. "Listen carefully. No more data drops. Someone hacked my security this morning. They know what I've been sending and they know your husband took the stuff. They'll be coming for him any time now, probably for you and your little girl too. You have to leave your house immediately."

With a click the line went dead.

*To keep reading, look for the novel at your favorite retailer in e-book or trade paperback editions.*

www.ingramcontent.com/pod-product-compliance
Lightning Source LLC
Chambersburg PA
CBHW021235250626
47155CB00008B/3025